WINTER PARK PUB
460 E. NEW ENGL
WINTER PARK, FLORIDA 32789

P9-CFJ-821

DISCARD

DARK
ROADS

H A R C O U R T   B R A C E   J O V A N O V I C H

DARK ROADS

LEAH ROSS

NEW YORK AND LONDON

F/8.

Copyright © 1975 by Leah Ross

All rights reserved. No part of this publication
may be reproduced or transmitted in any form or
by any means, electronic or mechanical, including
photocopy, recording, or any information storage
and retrieval system, without permission in
writing from the publisher.

Printed in the United States of America

The lines from "The Nitty Gritty" quoted on page 15 are
copyright © 1963 by Al Gallico Music Corp., international
copyright secured, all rights reserved, used by permission.

Library of Congress Cataloging in Publication Data
Ross, Leah.
  Dark Roads
  1. Title.   1. Florida – Fiction.
PZ4.R82345Dar   [PS3568.08435]   813'.5'4   75-1213
ISBN 0-15-123890-1

First edition

B C D E

FOR MY FATHER
IN MEMORIAM
AND WITH GRATITUDE,
FOR THE KING
IN LOVE
AND SPLENDOR,
AND
FOR MY SON
A SCIENTIST
AND
A DREAMER

CONNIE WILDER

She saw herself as a picture in *The Family of Man* . . . a slim ten-year-old girl sitting on a rock playing the recorder, with her hair whipped back over her shoulder by the wind. . . . She saw herself in terms of her guitar, that other limb of her body, and in terms of dance, those fervent liquid motions through which her body became itself. The flowering of art within her, though she had never wholly pursued it, *was* her . . . the intellect she studied with she tried to keep knife-blade sharp, but dance and the guitar and the girl on the rock were her very soul and being. . . .

PART ONE

INTIMATIONS

In her dreams, she imagined a new life; her imagination redrew what she saw during the day so that whatever future she and Alan had became luminous . . . in her dreams, it did not matter where they went, because she seemed so wholly included . . . when she awoke, and the dream disappeared, she felt that he was making his decision by himself. . . .

At the turn in her life that she now found herself moving through, she liked living in Berkeley . . . she liked living close to San Francisco, to sophistication and bookstores and radical politics and coffeehouses. She had given birth to two children under the vague impression that Alan would always be a graduate student and that they'd always live in Berkeley . . . even though she'd known that this wasn't so. . . .

Now he had his law degree . . . that had been the goal of years of study . . . well, he said, she'd gotten used to Berkeley and she'd get used to another place, but it had taken her six years to get used to Berkeley after New York!

In the high, lighted space that was the living room of their apartment, she sat on the window seat and looked out through the banked windows at the familiar activity of Grove Street. . . . Cars and students riding bicycles with their Harvard green bags slung over their shoulders, all of it evoking the heavy taste of nostalgia in her mouth.

Alan was in the process of deciding between Boston and Orangedale, Florida, a bleak small Southern town that no one had ever heard of. Her friend Sally Krause said she knew that Connie could never survive Orangedale and suggested Boston . . . but Connie knew that Orangedale offered more to Alan. . . . Expectations, you geared your life to what you looked forward to and what you had accomplished. What would they accomplish if they went to Orangedale, Florida. . . . Alan said, Go to graduate school and get a masters. Maybe.

She sat on the window seat with her arms curled around her legs; her body was slim, like an undergraduate's, a dancer's body, and she wore her hair long, in a ponytail, like theirs, but she was over thirty, almost a professor's wife. . . . She needed to go downstairs and pick up Willie and Robin from the neighbors'. She needed to be at the Co-op buying something for dinner. . . . Sally had said, If you go to Orangedale, all your friends will be black. Hardly, she'd replied, for she was sure that all the people there, black and white, could not possibly interest her, for her people were city people.

The Co-op was crowded. They drove three times around the parking lot before they could find a parking place. The Co-op was at the very center of her way of life. . . . She couldn't imagine that Orangedale, Florida would have any way of knowing what a Co-op was . . . the rich, dark health-food bread they bought, brown rice and cracked wheat, the art classes the kids had upstairs, the gourmet shelf from which she purchased the indispensable ingredients for her fancy dishes . . . time past and gone, the memory of something wonderful that she knew she couldn't have any more. . . .

Banging her cart along the aisles of the Co-op, her son hanging on to the front of the cart, hitching a ride, and her honey-haired daughter sitting in the cart seat, the three of them stopped, mesmerized, watching a man spray the lettuces with water so that their leaves stood out, glistening with the fresh drops, escarolle and head lettuce and butter lettuce and endives. There were cherries and strawberries and now the baked goods . . . and the specter of the South gleamed just beyond all the known wonders of the Co-op. . . . She met people she knew, people she liked and didn't like, and she stood with her foot up on the bottom rack of the cart and talked . . . yes, Alan was all through, yes they were leaving in less than a month, well no he hadn't decided yet . . . it would be either Boston or Orangedale, Florida. Well, it was somewhere in Florida. A Florida state college was there. . . . In the inner reaches of herself . . . Now I move among loved objects and loved faces and, above all, known worlds, there I shall be more alien than I have yet imagined it possible to be. . . .

Connie Wilder . . . combing her long, dark hair, distracted, staring out the window of their bedroom at the lone dark pine, rising against the darkening sky, the same pine she'd watched night after night while she'd sat on their bed nursing Robin, feeling the pull of the child on her nipple, feeling the growth of the dark tree outside . . . voices in the living room while she tied her hair into a dark knot.

"Mr. Wilder says to hurry, Mrs. Wilder." Jeannie's head appeared at the door. To Connie she looked like a child, but she wasn't; she was almost out of high school. They went into the children's room together, Jeannie chattering, Connie nodding as if she were listening.

"We're leaving now," Connie said to them. "Be good to Jeannie." They crashed against her, their soft, warm bodies leaning into her as they said good-bye. She kissed them, smoothed the hair away from their faces, and felt the intensity of their closeness; there was a level at which they seemed never to have become separate from her body, for when she held them, they seemed to melt into her.

She closed the door softly, a world closed off, and she went into the grown-up one wondering how she would prepare her children for the world ahead when she knew so little. . . .

Leaving the movie with its heaviness upon her, all the fashionable, depressing movies they saw, were almost obliged to see in order to keep up with their friends . . . They were on a steep narrow street in the expensive part of San Francisco, and the car was parked blocks below them. Graham and Sally were running down the hill ahead of them, racing and laughing, and she wanted to follow, to run and race and loose her hair upon the wind, but Alan had a headache from the movie, and so she walked with him and watched Sally, somehow a fragment of her past, a vision of herself eleven years before, racing down the New York streets when they'd left Grand Central Station. . . .

. . . They were the emissaries of good will, or so they had designated themselves. During the summer, the program they worked with sent underprivileged children from the city to camp, and they organized the trips, sent the kids out, met them and took them home if their parents weren't there. And so they spent half their nights and half their days at Grand Central, in the well of Pennsylvania Station, or at the Port Authority Bus Terminal. There were four of them: Luvenia McCray, a slim black girl who was a senior at Radcliffe and married, two facts that impressed Connie mightily, Bernard Levine, a Brooklyn Jewish boy who planned to study law and be a poet, Juan de la Torres, a Puerto Rican boy brought up in Hell's Kitchen, and herself, with her no ancestry and her tumble of desires to be a dancer, a folk singer and a saver of the world.

Now it was two in the morning, and they ran, raced up the dark, deserted street toward the Center, where Juan lived and they all worked. It had rained, and their sneakers slapped against the wet sidewalk, and the light from the streetlamps flickered crazily against brown cement. New York at 2:00 A.M., it was their city, their playground, with almost all of the millions of people sucked off the streets into their homes; only the heroic wandered the streets until dawn.

They played tag, up and down the steps of the brownstones, and Bernard caught Luvenia in a doorway at the top of the

7

stairs, caught her and held her, lightly, against the door. Connie, hearing Juan run down the street in another direction, followed the others up the stairs, and so as she stood halfway up, exhausted and breathing hard, heard Bernard ask Luvenia: "If I touched you, would we drown?"

"Yes, honey, so don't."

Connie backed down the stairs to the street; they hadn't known she was there, and she felt embarrassed at having been there, confused. Luvenia was married.

Later, the four of them gathered in the gym at the Center, and Luvenia put *"Tzena, Tzena"* on the record player, and they came together from the four corners of the earth and danced the hora. It was an old ritual; later, they'd sing, bum cigarettes from each other and drink beer until dawn.

They danced with their arms on each other's shoulders, around each other's necks, forming a circle, more and more dependent on each other as the music continued, bound in the circle of their convictions, their love, and Connie felt rather than saw all that went on between Bernard and Luvenia while they danced, and they danced freedom, all of them danced freedom, and for as long as she could remember when they danced or when they sang, their message was a total commitment to freedom....

They had reached the bottom of the steep hill, where Sally and Graham were waiting for them.

"Where were you?" Alan asked her.

"Oh, somewhere way in the past." She didn't want to share it with him, because she couldn't possibly convey the intensity of it; it was just Sally and Graham running down the hill the way *they* used to run....

"Let's go to the Coffee Cantata," Sally. The Coffee Cantata, where the tables were sleek, low and austere, where huge globes of light hung from the ceiling, the coffee was expensive and the music that surged through your conversation was classical.

Vivaldi. A violin concerto, the rich, thick sensuousness of violins . . . They sat on one of the low benches and ordered capuccino, *cioccolata* and baklava. When the waitress brought the porcelain cups and the tiny diamond-shaped pastries swimming in honey, Connie had another wrench . . . she might get tired of the Coffee Cantata, sometimes compare it unfavorably with the Village coffeehouses, but its beauty and wholeness were like that of a painting; it would be bound to strike you if you were going to a place where there would be no paintings at all.

"Don't you love Vivaldi?" Sally, between sips of the sweet chocolate. There were times when Connie felt possessive about *her* artists and didn't want to share them with anyone, not even Sally.

"Yes, Vivaldi's the only really life-giving classical music." Ridiculous to say, she knew, but it moved Vivaldi away from Sally and back to her.

"Connie, that's absurd." Alan laughed and looked at her affectionately, as if she were a child.

"No, it isn't. Vivaldi is music to make love by or have a baby by," building on the absurdity and yet telling her own version of the truth from one of her deeper levels . . . it almost always got her into trouble.

"You could say the same thing about any classical composer," Graham Geisman. Then he went on to make a generalization about Vivaldi's themes in relation to Bach's, and she stopped listening, and they put on a Bach cantata, and she withdrew into her own thoughts. . . . Vivaldi, one of the threads that knotted her to her past . . .

. . . "Will you turn that record player down!" The door of Connie's room opened, and her mother stood there, fat and slightly stoop-shouldered in a pink dress. "Your father and I can hardly hear ourselves think." And she split the spell wide open; Vivaldi had been drowning the walls, the music rising and breaking over the room, and she had been lying thousands of feet under water and hearing and seeing and smelling it.

"Mother, it has to be played this way, it's Vivaldi."

"I know very well what it is. Half the people in the apartment house know. How could they help it? It's louder than the bus." It's louder than the bus. What kind of a statement was that to make. Whenever she was in the midst of some great experience, her mother had to reduce it to something like the noise of a bus. "Really, Connie, you've got to keep that record player down. This is an apartment house, not the Central Park Zoo."

"Mother, you can't hear it when it's soft. It's not the same. You miss it all."

"You're always so intense about everything," her mother's voice drifting back to her as her mother returned to the living room, where she repeated the remark to her father.

And a few minutes later, as she was pulling her heavy, dark-blue seaman's sweater on, down over her jeans, she heard her mother's voice again.

"Connie, Robert is here," the disapproval there in the voice and then the murmur of their conversation. Robert was deliberately, obscurely intellectual, and to her mother, he represented everything that spoke of instability. He seldom had even enough money to buy his subway tokens; that was the thing her mother always mentioned. She could feel her mother leaning toward a certain kind of boy for her already, one who would support her, who was reliable. Robert was not reliable even by her own standards. He also dressed to shock and hit it every time with her mother. Tonight he was wearing his rust brown corduroy jacket, a light green shirt, dark blue pants and a lavender tie.

"Have a good time. Be back by 12:30." Her father had not yet accustomed himself to the fact that she dated at all. Her mother was more ambitious about her prospects, her father was more old-fashioned.

"Come on, Robert." She was angry at him herself tonight because he was late and because he looked so stupid when she looked so nice, all dark blue and bohemian with her guitar and her long ponytail. Sometimes he drove her crazy.

"Now remember, Robert"—as he opened the front door— "she's only sixteen."

With the close of the door as she pressed the elevator button: "My God, she says that every single goddam time we leave."

"I know, but she worries about me. How come you're so late?"

He looked at his watch. "I'm only two hours late. I was writing a poem." She felt the fight coming and avoided it.

"Can I hear it?"

He recited it in the elevator and explicated it all the way to the Village:

Now
In time's mind's eye
Beyond some dull Eternity's
Edge
I find a formal explanation
Of love's momentary
Jerk and pause
And gasp
To fill
That space
Created
By time's
Void

When they got off the subway in the Village, she still didn't understand it, but she was drunk on his renditions.

They walked the dark streets of the Village, and he talked on: visions of the artist's intellect, Yeats, Eliot, Pound, W. S. Merwin and X. J. Kennedy, and her guitar banged rhythmically against her hip. At Rienzi's they ordered one dinner, beef with noodles, two plates, and a pot of coffee. Intimacy felt and achieved by Robert shoving half his beef and noodles onto her plate with his fork. And later, as people gathered around, she played her guitar and sang songs of oppression and freedom, thinking of her parents on Central Park West, of her mother's hand on the lamp switch.

"Ready for bed, Harold?" businesslike, the same sentence every night. She wondered if her parents ever made love any more and doubted it; they were probably too old.

She sat at the brown, scarred table on a heavy wooden chair and sang, drawing her circle around her toward the light of the candle on their table. Now the candle burned among empty coffee cups and plates stained with beef and noodles, now she watched the faces, changed and softened by the candlelight, each of them somehow in his own world, each of them giving his own depth and meaning to the song. . . .

And, later, after the Coffee Cantata, when she and Alan were at home getting undressed for bed, he said, "Wouldn't it be strange if it turned out that you liked it in Orangedale?"

She watched him throw his dirty clothes into a pile on the floor and toss the pants he would wear tomorrow over the back of a chair. He was so careful about his legal work and so sloppy around the house. . . .

"That would be impossible," she replied, and felt her vehemence shake her; she didn't feel comfortable letting him too far into her world; it was just not part of their life together.

They were going to Orangedale, Florida, a bleak small Southern town that no one had ever heard of. . . .

FLASHFORWARD

*And always when she looked back,
she wondered at the way the decision
was made, and at the decision itself.
Retrospect cast a long shadow over
one's sense of one's self, retrospect
explained and demanded growth, and
fate somehow ultimately took care.
Or so it seemed later.*

CHAPTER 2

Parties. Gatherings of friends. Ten o'clock. The light bulbs were red and blue and green and rubbed soft nightclub light up the walls. In the living room, the light was lavender, the punch bowl was full of heavy rum punch. There were wooden platters of bread and cheese and salami, and wooden bowls of pretzels and nuts and potato chips. Shirley Ellis on the record player:

Some folks know about it, some don't
Some will learn to shout it, some won't
But sooner or later, baby . . .

She could feel the beat of the music in her bones, but there were only a few people there, and no one was dancing. In their bedroom, they'd put a big table with a roulette wheel, and Sally Krause sat in the children's room swathed in a red sari, reading fortunes from a pack of cards she'd picked up in a café in Paris. Willie and Robin were spending the night with Sally's parents in the city, and the house belonged wholly to the party. The dress she'd bought for the party was pink and purple, soft chiffon, floating folds, and when she raised her arm, her gold Indian bracelets fell together with a sound like the tinkling of a series of tiny bells. Fling one last perfect atmosphere over her friends before she and Alan left. They were not going, after all, to Boston, they were going to Florida, to some obscure swamp place, and she didn't plan ever to make any more friends, not like these.

She moved through the party as if she were some spirit, animating it but not wholly there. People were dancing now, and she danced with Alan's office mate and made poised moments of academic conversation . . . she drank three paper cups full of the strong, sweet punch, feeling her body slim and graceful under the softness of the dress, ready to dance . . . life and love . . . joy and disaster . . . the feel of the punch sliding down her throat. She wanted everyone at the party she cared about. . . .

People were beginning to loosen up, and they played a game where you wrote down who or what you would most like to be on a slip of paper. She moved among them collecting the slips of paper so that Alan could read them aloud, and she gazed at her friends as if they were characters in a play that had just ended for her.

Alan came up behind her. "Make sure that they say interesting things on those cards, or the game won't be funny. Help them out a little." She looked at him; it was against her principles. "It's going well, don't you think?" He was watching their guests, not noting her reactions.

"Yes," she said, thinking how their responses to things were always so different . . . she could be thinking of her friends as characters in a play and still feel herself one of them. He just watched. She went over to where her favorite professor, George Cronin, was talking with another professor about the game. "Put down that you want to be Connie's lover, George."

Connie collected the slips of paper from people near them.

"He just said that because that's what he wants to be," George, with a slow, subtle smile . . . the merest flicker of feeling between a man and a woman, but there was no place for it in the world in which they lived. . . .

She got up and went through the gambling salon, green light, and one man transformed by a green eyeshade into a big-time gambler . . . and she went into the room where Sally was reading fortunes, and she felt that she was intruding upon something holy even though she knew Sally was no fortune-teller.

"The cards tell me that you joke about all the mysteries of life," Sally to the fat lawyer.

"I do joke a lot," he said, looking worried.

Connie walked out. The cards tell me that you joke about all the mysteries of life, joke, think about, discuss intellectually but never seek to understand. It seemed to her that they all did that, but what else was there?

She came back into the living room just as someone put on a new stack of records, and she heard the first drumbeats and knew that the record of the three African bands was on; it was Lydia's record. She'd played it the night before and danced to it and thought they mustn't put it on at the party because it

16

moved her so deeply that she wasn't sure she would be able to stand it.

But it was on now, and she saw Lydia, slender and dark, swaying and clapping her hands to it, and she moved out with her to the center of a circle and began dancing, five feet from Lydia, independent, feeling the presence of the circle of people around her but only dimly aware of where they were, only knowing her link to the music and the forces that were her very soul, the beat, the step, what was beyond her body and the music, something of unity and ecstasy that you couldn't discuss but only be. . . .

"She's going to be a great shock to the state of Florida," George Cronin's voice, from the magic circle that they'd drawn around themselves . . .

Later, at 4:00 A.M., there were only four or five people left, and they did the hora on the empty paper-strewn floor to the music of *"Habe Naghilah"* until they were exhausted, and she and Alan let the last of the guests out and fell across the children's beds still dressed and went to sleep.

That was the last party they ever gave in Berkeley.

CHAPTER 3

There was a stasis in the atmosphere. The heat slid through everything. The town was layered in it, laden with it and buried by it. They had never sweated so much. They moved in, settled, as it were, and Alan started work as a faculty member at the Florida law school.

Connie tried to find things to do; she followed a series of complex channels to reach the Women's Civil Rights League, and they put her on a committee. Her whole sense of anticipation rested in that committee meeting. She was on the hospital committee, and they were to try to get medical facilities integrated. The doctors had two waiting rooms, one for "Colored," one for "White," and the hospital had one floor where all the black patients were put. Her sense that she might be able to accomplish something through the Women's Civil Rights League didn't shake her hatred of Orangedale though. They'd been here six weeks, and she felt the weight of it like a year.

Yet there was beauty in the land. At the end of the road, there was a leaf-drawn tunnel, coolness and darkness, as different from her life as shadow from sun. She wanted to walk through it, but it was not her tunnel—the dark children walked down it barefoot, a slow dance into the fern-fringed, sun-slid green of the tunnel; the sun filtered through the leaves, throwing light onto the dark skin of the children. Her longing was for dark earth, a dampness, a feel beneath bare feet. . . .

In the South grew flowers: thick clusters of lavender, heavy white blossoms bursting upward, great trees rising with pink-fringed flowers on their branches, and honeysuckle with its heavy smells, a deep, sensual atmosphere, its surface flower-laden and the layers beneath, like roots in damp earth, enriching it. . . .

She wrote it all in letters to Sally Krause, who hopped on a plane within three weeks of the day they had arrived so she could make the Orangedale scene on her way to Miami. . . .

"There's no scene, Sally," Connie said when she met her at the small landing strip that Orangedale called an airport. "It's simply dead, no war, no nothing."

19

"There must be a spade scene," Sally said, "and a little beat scene. It's the South and a university town. Must be." Connie shrugged. Sally found a bar that was full of homosexuals and pot within a week.

"You see," Sally said as they sat at The Bar and drank beer, "a really good homosexual scene, fags of all varieties simply hanging from the wall." Connie felt chagrined that she hadn't known about it before. She'd been too intent on the remains of the despised system and too miserable. At any rate, this scene bored her now, and she wondered if she was getting old . . . once she'd been bohemian, Connie Bartlett, now she felt the disappearance of that whole identity.

"Mediocre pot," she said to Sally, who'd passed her a joint. . . . Yes, they had made the grand scenes, colleges and New York and San Francisco, and she and Sally had been best friends for as long as she could remember. Now she was thirty-one and married, she had two children and she was halfway respectable; Sally was rich and still making scenes. The similarities between them were fading. When Connie looked below the fictional Southern surface, she saw and felt only agony, and most of the things she'd felt and done before she came here seemed irrelevant.

She and Alan discussed Sally the night before Sally went on to Miami.

"A rich, out-of-touch innocent," Alan said.

Connie thought of the envy she felt of Sally now. "She's very free," she said.

"And very uncommitted, to use your favorite word."

He was right, she knew that. What she envied most in Sally's freedom was her ability to leave Orangedale while she herself had been given an indeterminate sentence. She turned off the light and climbed into bed beside Alan. There was not the sound of a car on the street, tonight not even a dog barking. They lay there listening to absolute silence, and she felt the heat waver outside and then fold over them, smothering them in some final blanket from which there was no escape.

Before Sally got onto the plane the next day, Connie asked her back.

"Okay," Sally said, "but next time I come, you've got to show me the spade scene."

That night Connie drove to the hospital committee meeting in a secluded, black middle-class section of town, Carver Heights, where the houses were set apart and had large lawns. The house she was supposed to go to was the largest house in the neighborhood, at the end of the street, you couldn't miss it, Mrs. Jenkins had said. She drove up the curved driveway; there were already several cars there, a Lincoln Continental, a Cadillac, a paneled station wagon, all of them expensive. She got out of the car slowly. The chances of her being accepted diminished . . . what she knew of the black middle class, she knew through books. One thing in America was that the three classes were lower, middle and rich; there was no upper. By this standard, the people in this house in front of her were rich.

And what did it all mean? The black middle class, rich and secure, would it just be the mirror image of what she had grown up with? In her past, somewhere, she had looked to black people for her spiritual education, for a richer perspective, Luvenia McCray . . . and Shirley Taylor in New York. . . .

. . . Picking the kids up at the train stations after they'd gone to camp, sending them out, she and Shirley Taylor and Lisa Villella, whom everyone referred to as "Villa." Shirley was slim and dark-skinned; she wore her black hair in a roll at the back of her neck with a hair net over it, like a waitress, and she always wore dark glasses. She worked with the Ninety-sixth Precinct, and her kids were recruited for camp right at the police station; she had six kids of her own, four dark girls and two Chinese boys, whom she said really belonged to a Chinese man who had returned to China to talk with his wife about leaving her to marry Shirley. Connie's boss said Shirley had a problem about race, was black but didn't want to admit it; Connie, loving Shirley and having no use for her boss, said she didn't think so and listened to Shirley weave tales of Indian ancestry, American or Indian Indian by turns, and tell of the voyage of

21

her Puerto Rican grandfather from his island to the United States.

Where Shirley was all imagination, Villa was all hard facts. She was short and hunchbacked and bony, and her skin had weathered to an almost dead white. Her hair too was white, and her eyes a startling bright blue. She was over seventy, and her love of realism had grown of necessity out of her experience ... the Spaniard whom she had loved to distraction had died early and left her a young widow. Searching for some way to continue her life, she had lodged herself in Chinatown, where she had started a home for abandoned Chinese children. Whenever Villa came to the station, she was surrounded by her children, who clung to her so closely that all their heads of dark shining hair seemed to grow out of her ... buds on the thin stem of her body. She smiled, and her whole being shone, light radiated out of her. She and Shirley had their Chinese children in common.

When Connie wasn't with Luvenia and Bernard and Juan, she usually ate in the station cafeteria with Shirley and Villa. They sat over hamburgers and coffee listening to Shirley.

"My fingers are so crippled with arthritis, I had to put my rings on the other hand." Flashing her diamond, "This may look real to you, but this one is a fake. Li-Cho told me to put the real one in the vault, the real one, y'see," she leaned over and stage-whispered, "the real one is hot, and Li-Cho said: 'Shirley,' he said, 'this stuff is just too hot to wear, so put it in the vault and when I get my wife straight, I'll be back and we'll live rich and you can wear the whole mess.'"

Villa, smiling all the while and puffing on her fifteenth cigarette of the day: "Shirley, you don't believe that man is coming back from China, do you?"

"Of course he is." Shirley sat back and lit a cigarette; she was thirty-five, but all the joints of her hands were swollen, her rings hung on her thin fingers beneath the swollen joints. "Of course he is." She wasn't even irritated, Connie thought, her faith in the power of her own visions was so great. . . .

But only three weeks later, she went to visit Shirley and found her sitting on the couch like a zombie, chain-smoking

22

while Lena, her oldest daughter, made lunch. Lena was twelve.

"I don' know what's the matter with Mama," Lena said, large intense eyes in a small, thin face. "I think it has something to do with Li-Cho, she heard from him today." She shook her head. "I never did think he was coming back from China."

Lena wanted to be a doctor. They talked about that.

"I can see you as a doctor," Connie said, Lena with her small steady hands, her mature and steady mind. They took plates of tuna-fish sandwiches and glasses of milk out to the children in the living room. Connie loved Shirley, but she could see how it would be difficult to be Shirley's daughter. Shirley's doctor had urged her to smoke because she had such bad nerves. So said Shirley.

Now she sat with her on the couch, and finally she broke, talked, brought out the whole tale of Li-Cho and his smuggling ventures. He had used her, now he wanted her to send his sons home. He must stay with his wife; it was a Chinese custom.

"Connie," Shirley said when the whole story had come out, "listen, Connie, and remember this. Love is what you feel for your children, and that's all. Love has nothing to do with men. What a man is good for is scratching your back when you're in the bathtub. . . . Don't ever let a man get to you, Connie, no matter what else you do or don't do." Connie nodded, more to calm Shirley than anything else. Lena stood in the doorway, just shaking her head, and Connie felt in Shirley's words the force of an incantation, Shirley older than thirty-five, Lena generations older than twelve.

It was people like Shirley and Villa who had formed her so far, brushing her life briefly, so briefly that it seemed as if they must have been shadow to the rest of her life's substance.

She rang the doorbell. She could hear voices inside the house.

"Hello, you must be Connie, you're the only new one." The girl who greeted her wasn't more than twenty, beautiful and heavily made-up. "Did you have trouble finding the house?"

"No." Connie shook her head. "It was easy. You gave good directions."

"It's the biggest, right?" Wilma Jenkins giggled. "My husband always says, 'Baby, I want it to be the biggest and the fanciest they got. I want people to *know* we got money.'" She laughed again. "We better get in there. We're holding the meeting up." Into the TV den, dim light, with one bright lamp and next to it a thin red-haired woman writing something in a notebook.

"This is Connie Wilder," Wilma was saying, and she went around the room; there were three black women besides Wilma and two white women, the one with the notebook and another one who looked like a gym teacher and kept running her hand through her hair. "Connie is the new member of our committee. She's from . . . ?" Wilma looked at her.

"California."

"That's a long way away," one of the older women said. "We certainly hope you'll like it here."

"Thank you."

"Now this meeting is going to have to come to order, or we're never going to get home and my husband simply won't allow that."

For a while, Connie just listened while they talked, and she studied the faces highlighted by the dim, indirect lighting. There was Wilma, with her round face; the thin red-haired woman; Linda Tweed, argumentative and intense, the gym teacher; the head of the group, an older black woman, and, finally, there was a nurse. While the others talked about the hospital and the medical center at the state college from hearsay, the nurse seemed to know both situations inside out and spoke with authority.

By the end of the meeting, they had decided they would send a questionnaire to the doctors in the town about their medical facilities and whether or not they were integrated, and they would get all the facts about the general hospital so that they could take some kind of legal action. Verena Greene, the nurse, volunteered to work on the hospital situation, and Connie volunteered to work with her.

They stood outside on the dark curved driveway and talked before they left.

"I live right over there." Verena gestured toward a much smaller house across the street. "When we get some facts on the hospital, we can meet over there."

Connie nodded. "Or we can meet at my house," and she told Verena where she lived, conscious of the delicate balance of the South, of black-white relationships, conscious that this was not New York and not Berkeley; Verena might think she would go to her house but not want the favor returned.

"Do you have any children?" Connie asked her.

"Yes, two boys, five and seven."

"I have a boy who's five; we should get them together." Verena nodded, but Connie had the feeling that Verena thought they never would.

She got into her car then and drove down a long stretch of empty street, thinking that if Orangedale held almost nothing for her, here at least was the possibility of a friendship.

CHAPTER 4

During the heat of that first summer in Orangedale, the Wilders were invited to the Swinburnes. Swinburne, G. M., was one of the two most prominent lawyers in Orangedale, and an invitation to the Swinburne home was a statement to the effect that you were either potentially desirable or potentially dangerous.

"I don't want to go," Connie said.

"I don't want to go either," Alan said, "but with the Swinburnes, it's not a matter of wanting to, it's a matter of a command performance." Her temperament resisted, but she put on a soft, cream-colored shirtwaist dress and ladylike high heels, and they went. Alan taught in the law school; she was a faculty wife.

The drive took them out of town, off the paved roads and into the woods. The Swinburnes lived at the edge of a lake, in the middle of deep trees where the moss hung thick. They had retreated into the comfortable hugeness of their own mansion: swirls of lawn and sports cars parked casually in the cut-rock gravel beds of the driveways. The blue diamond of the swimming pool cut into the lawn, one tip of it almost in the lake where swamp grass grew long and curved against the short, rough green of the lawn and a small boat rose and fell briefly next to a pier that was attached to the patio of Swinburne Hall (as the place announced itself on the mailbox).

"Welcum, welcum," Mrs. Swinburne, with a face cut as sharply as the diamond-shaped pool, her hair in a graceful swirled bun, her dress white, casual, her feet in sandals, a Southern version of one of the women in *The New Yorker* ads. "Come in, come in, and this is yoah wahf, Mistuh Wahlduh; ahm so pleased to meet huh." And Connie shook the cold hand that was offered to her, looking into cold gray-blue eyes that were not looking into hers.

They advanced into the sunken living room, Swinburne gave them drinks and a black maid dressed in a black uniform with a white apron entered carrying a plate of hors d'oeuvres, which she passed around. The living room had light, space, design, and a high ceiling. Connie was sitting on a couch, and the maid brought her the platter. Connie looked into her eyes, deep brown, and felt her image reflected in the woman's eyes, her feelings lurking somewhere inside the woman's skin, the woman's feelings inside hers, but she knew they couldn't be. She knew the game, the white liberal's superficial knowledge of what black people felt, a game for members of the Women's Civil Rights League, but there was something that seemed to be passing between her and that woman, and then finally she took a round of toast from the tray, and the tray moved, and the moment vanished. She was sitting there, and the conversation that she heard at a distance but knew to be going on right around her was as brittle as the glass in her hand, and the vision in her mind rose to the touch, palpable, more palpable than the cracker with a smear of orange cheese on it in her hand.

Mrs. Swinburne, referred to by the younger women in the room as "Miss Cora," started toward the kitchen.

"Now ahm goin' intuh the kitchen. All you ladies just cum in and join me." They rose from their chairs like so many robots and followed, Connie feeling caught in their motion, turning to look for Alan, wanting to tell him she was drowning, but she saw him busy talking to other lawyers. She was, after all, a woman, this was her job, and there was for her no neutral ground. She was put deeply, solidly in conjunction with other women's personalities. She could blow up, erupt like a volcano, or drown in the intensity of her own feelings and keep silent. He talked law while she had visions.

She walked into the kitchen, where the women sat or stood around the room like so many decorations, flowered in their dresses, slender in their figures, vacant in their eyes. The maid moved with ease around the kitchen, a world she controlled so that her every gesture described her mastery. Connie stood with her back to a wall wondering . . . what must she think of us? There was, Connie felt, between herself and Mrs. Swinburne's people a square of air-burdened space. The white women there had shadowed eyelids with panes of opaque glass beneath, their eyes decorative, enclosing vaults, the spaces where their souls might have been.

Mrs. Swinburne made kitchen gestures, rearranging crackers on a tray while the maid stood behind her, waiting for her to finish, so that she could sweep the tray off the table and carry it into the other room.

"Now let me tell you what happened today," Mrs. Swinburne. "Ah have made this cake mennih tahmes, and ah have never made a mistake makin' it. This mohnin' ah was makin' it, an' the yahd man was doin' the yahd, and he got thirsty an' came to the back door, an' they-uh he stood, all hot an' thirsty-lookin'." The maid came back into the kitchen, and by her very lack of pressure, by her silence and her swift movements, made Mrs. Swinburne suddenly seem awkward and superfluous. "He looked like he was goin' to have a haht attack, and ah was so worried that ah gave him a glass of watuh an' then when ah went back to mah cake, ah was so rattled that ah forgot a cup of flouwuh. It was terrible." The ladies laughed, the laughter of crystal shattering on cement.

Connie left them and walked unsteadily out to the patio. Across the lake a sunset was beginning, rose pinks and oranges flooding the sky, a film of color spreading in the distance and, beneath it, the peaceful silence of the lake and the graceful grasses curving up into the colored spaces. Behind her, Miss Cora's voice cut like a dozen knives into her feeling of color.

"Ah'm Janice." Connie turned from the lake to a girl who sat in the chair next to hers. The girl's skin was tanned, soft café au lait, she had large, soft brown eyes, and her hair fell in waves and curls, brown blond, corn-silk hair, her dress was coral-colored, and her sandals revealed delicate, vulnerable feet. Her movements were languid, they spoke of leisure, the real thing, the Southern belle incarnate. "Ah declayuh, ah'm so tahred."

"What sort of work do you do?" Tension in her voice, knowing it to be a New York–Berkeley question.

"Work?" The word crossed the girl's tongue as if for the first time. Her mouth explored its possibilities. "Just housework," her lovely manicured hands belying the statement. "Just help the maid with the housework," her hands playing with a handkerchief in her lap, and Connie thought how, despite her beauty, she looked like nothing so much as a child who wasn't wholly bright. "Miss Cora shuah can cook," turning her head so that the hair fell gracefully away from her neck as Miss Cora wheeled the food out onto the patio: cold jellied madrilène, lobster salad, thin slices of bread with butter.

"Just a little suppah, c'mon all you men. Give up your lil' ol' talk and eat." And as the men came back to the patio, Miss Cora suddenly became joyous, direct, energetic, vibrant. . . .

On the way home, they were silent for a long time. Connie knew that Alan didn't want to talk because he knew how she felt and yet knew further that Swinburne would be important to him here and might even be essential. She was simply seething, hatred and sickness welling up in her. Finally she spoke.

"I don't *ever* want to have money," thinking of all the corruption and decay at the Swinburnes'.

Alan sighed, an audible expulsion of his breath. "Well, if I ever should get a job where I was making money, then we would have it," careful, as if he hoped to avoid some explosion he expected to follow.

"Well, I don't *want* you to get a job like that; it's obscene, and if you ever do, we'll just give all our money away." He didn't want to talk more, she knew, and if she talked more, she would simply start on the black-white thing and the total ineptness and ignorance of white people who let black people do their work for them and had nothing more to talk about than giving the yard man a glass of water. She could feel her blood rising and pressing against her skin, and he was sitting there, driving, God *knew* what he was thinking, but he was just sitting there while she thought she might explode or die or both within the next five seconds.

By the time they got home, it was after twelve. She hadn't realized how many hours they'd been there, even though it had seemed like it would never end; the whole thing had had a timeless quality. She switched the light on in their bedroom, and the room—bed, desk, chair—was suddenly lighted, square and comfortable. I live, she thought, in an agony of intention. She was waiting, not out of fear, but because they lived in a strange country here, the strangest she'd ever been in, and she didn't yet know how to get to the center of it. . . .

CHAPTER 5

Six months of Orangedale . . . she sat at Kay Levy's house; Kay was her other friend. Kay and Verena held her together through the long, hard depressions that formed the thread of continuity in her life. She watched Kay now as she made coffee, Kay, who was small and energetic, with her short, dark hair and thin face, Kay, who dressed as if she were going downtown in New York rather than to the supermarket in Orangedale. . . .

At Kay's they drank coffee and ate bagels with cream cheese, at Verena's they drank Kool-Aid and Coca-Cola, and at both places they sat and discussed the problems of the world but more particularly the problem of living in Orangedale, Florida.

Connie and Kay had met over the phone when Kay, in an attempt to make the world better and to force herself to live in Orangedale in a constructive manner, had been spending most of her time organizing volunteers to drive people to the courthouse so that they could register to vote. When Kay had called her, her voice and attitude had been so clearly New York that they had fallen into a three-hour conversation, prompting Alan to ask, when she finally got off, "Who in hell was that?"

"Kay Levy," she'd replied. "She's from New York, and she's Jewish."

"Two thousand points for Kay Levy," but then he smiled. "Hey, it was good to hear you talk that long on the phone again."

This immediately reminded her that she was, as it were, permanently depressed, and she sighed. "Well, she might turn out to be my friend, and then I'd have two."

Alan shook his head, and she knew why. For Alan, two friends would be sufficient, but at the hard, rewarding center of his life was his work, and it was a solid center when his work was going well . . . if only she'd liked graduate school, she told herself, if, if, if; her life broke itself down into a series of unhappy hypotheses.

They sat at the round yellow table in Kay's kitchen, with their coffee cups before them, and discussed the situation.

"You know what I'd like to do," Connie said. Kay shook her head. "I'd like to start a dance class for black kids. I had that idea when we were in Berkeley, and I've talked about it here, but I haven't gotten much response." There were fires of inspiration within her when she thought about one of her projects, a wave of energy that rose and guided her to action; she could walk on it and breathe in it, and it broke and fell only when her action had been completed.

"I'd be willing to help you organize it; I'll bet you could get one of the recreation centers to dance in. They're supposed to be for city use. I'm going to call Christine Duval; she helped with the voter registration drive. I bet she'd know how to get it organized," and Kay pulled the receiver of the phone down and dialed while she sat at the table drinking coffee . . . a New York way to do things, prompt, efficient and fast, thought translated into action the moment it hit the air . . . she listened to Kay talk on the phone absently, and the original image she'd had in Berkeley returned to her . . . she'd been in the living room of their apartment doing casual choreography to a Peter, Paul and Mary record, "Very Last Day," and the image had come to her . . . the girls were young, slim, dark, and they wore black leotards and black tights, and there were maybe twelve of them on stage, and the guitar chords banged out the beats of freedom, and the girls turned and swung, and one of them melted into the floor and rose again, and the music was through her and of her . . . and the beauty of it had stopped Connie's heart for a moment, and she'd thought, I'll do that, and now . . . the translation into action . . .

Kay hung up the phone. "Christine says she'll be glad to help you get started. She thinks we can get a recreation center for it, and she'll speak to the man in charge of them. She also said she's got a fifteen-year-old daughter, Jane, and that she'd like to have her in it because Jane's very interested in dance . . . so how's that? She said she'd call you in a couple of days."

"Great." The image re-formed itself in her mind. . . . "I'd better go home and practice," she said to Kay. "I'm out of shape." Kay got up with her as she collected her keys and purse, and walked her to the door. "Thanks," Connie said.

"It was nothing; you're the one who's going to have to do all the work."

On the living-room rug . . . she was curled up, doing her bounces, stretching her legs, learning her neglected muscles all over again . . . she was suddenly aware of every muscle in her body, the ache and the pull and the stretch, the beauty of the body's moments in space when she leaped, the agony of an exercise when the body was unready. . . .

She sat in the backyard, the sweat soaking through her leotard, and watched Willie try to teach Robin how to throw a football. . . . It was December, but most days were warm, and the kids were out in shorts and T-shirts. . . . With her sense of the dance class ahead of her, watching her children play, their laughter breaking against the clear air, she felt happy, as if she and her own nature were suddenly and wholly together, as if her nature blended with that larger concept of nature that included all there was of creation. . . . In the yard, half grass and half dirt, her children played, and Robin came and rested her small, fat body against her mother's knees, Robin sweaty and dirty and like any other of nature's small wild animals. . . . She put her hands on Robin's head, through the soft silkiness of Robin's hair, half gold, half orange, unbelievable hair, and it seemed to her that her two children, with their closeness to nature and to earth, were at some point where people should stay . . . the complications of life when it got away from nature seemed to her unnecessary. . . .

Willie climbed a tree in the backyard, and she watched him, his small legs gripping the trunk of the tree, and he too was the tree. . . . In the South, you were drawn to nature, surrounded by it, and if you weren't strong enough, drowned in it, nature and your nature. She stared at the tree Willie was on, and the trunk and shape of the tree seemed suddenly to attain another dimension, and she felt herself as a part of the tree, an experience as different from that of seeing Willie as a part of the tree as the experience of water was different from the experience of land . . . the ripe time of withdrawal into nature and into yourself. . . . Something would happen here, she was sure, maybe something she wasn't ready for. . . .

But the mood and the moment passed. In the kitchen, there was chicken to be cut up and fried for supper, there was school-work to be done afterward. What she had felt in the yard was completely gone now, and she could only vaguely remember that fifteen minutes before she had felt it. Nature here was beautiful, thick and tropical, but it was not her landscape; it was so alien to her that she often wanted to shut it out or to shut herself in. She felt within her a sense of deadness, the urge to destroy. There was nature, but it was a slick cover for racism; there was no spring, no time of rebirth and arousal, only the heat. If you were civilized, and she was sure she was, there was no way you could live here.

Boredom, tedium, the harsh blinding atmosphere of her permanent melancholy . . . the dance class, the moment outside, and then her depression claimed her as startlingly and completely as if she'd been struck on the head and gone un-conscious. Robin came in and sat close to the kitchen table watching her make fried chicken, one fat elbow on the table, her fist on her chin and a damp curl stuck against her fore-head, and Connie gazed at her, wondering, Why do we do it to them, why do we bear them and bring them into a meaning-less world, promising ourselves when we marry that we'll do it differently, that we won't make the same mistakes our parents made and then making them?

She was fixing drinks when Alan came in. He pulled off his jacket, loosened his tie and rolled up his shirt sleeves.

"Just what I need." He took the drink and kissed her.

"I knew it would be. You're working too hard."

"I have to; in addition to all the regular stuff, Joseph Lansing takes his bar exam in a week and I promised to help him."

"That was nice of you."

"Well, I have to. He's nervous as a cat; he knows the material backwards and forwards, but he needs reassurance, and drilling seems to give him confidence. I was the same way, and if

Harvey hadn't helped me . . ." He took a sip of his drink. "You look good, thinner or something."

"I danced today." She told him about the dance class, and he was pleased, something to occupy her time. They spoke to each other as if from the depths of some common experience, but she felt it wasn't real. He went to the law school every day and came home, and he thought it was real. Maybe it was, for him. But for her . . . He felt that his life was whole, that their life was whole, that the only changes that needed to be made were surface changes. Dance class would do it all, get her out of the house more, since graduate school hadn't been the answer. *The* answer. She knew obscurely but absolutely that there wasn't any answer, but she felt something at the center of her in need of change. There was no way that she could explain to him what had happened to her in the backyard, and she didn't even want to try; she didn't even understand it herself; she had absolutely no sense of why her moods changed, but she'd felt intimations, as if some moment in her future had condescended to land briefly in the confusion of her present, just intimations. . . .

They sat in the living room eating cheese and crackers and drinking. He put on a Mozart symphony and sat back. She liked it too, but somehow the constant background of Mozart, the constant mind games they played with their friends or acquaintances, the rounds of drinks, the rounds of melba toast and sesame-seed crackers with cheese or clam dip or onion dip . . .

"What are you thinking about?" toward the end of the second movement.

"Why?" He monitored her thoughts, and she didn't like it. "You looked so far away."

"I was thinking how I'd like to go to the drive-in tonight." He picked up the paper and opened it to the movie page.

"Nothing much on. *Tammy and the Doctor* at one, horror show at the other."

"Well, I'll see *Tammy and the Doctor*. I'd see anything except the horror show, in order to get out of the house." He looked at her.

"All right," he said. "We can go after dinner if you get the kids ready."

At the drive-in, she and Alan sat holding hands, and the children jumped and fussed in the back, and they went back and forth to the canteen for sticky, bubbly drinks that were bad for their stomachs and teeth, with popcorn that got spilled on the floor and with sweet chocolate. *Tammy and the Doctor* was worse than they'd expected, and she found herself wondering idly what it would be like to go to bed with the men in the picture, one after another, as they were flashed onto the screen, and none of them really attracted her. It was all idle speculation, everything was, and then . . . the rising of her mind's most central thought . . . there must be more to life than this.

CHAPTER 6

A pattern of heart-shaped leaves against a purple-black sky, like someone putting his hand on her heart to slow her down. It was the first night of dance class. Christine Duval and Kay had done a lot of the organization, and she was supposed to have ten girls in her class to start with, ten girls whom Christine said were really interested in dance. As she drove, her mind dropped into memories . . . Wanda Williams, the original half-conscious source of inspiration for her dance class, the unspoken debts you owed to people who had influenced your life in so profound a way that you almost might not speak of it.

"One, two, three, four, lift your legs and extend, five, six, seven, eight, straighten them out to the side, nine, ten, eleven, twelve, leg extension to the back . . ." Mrs. Lowry walking back and forth while she guided them in their exercises, the spinet piano overly loud, the sound somehow broken as Mrs. Watson, their music teacher, pounded it out. The room they danced in had varnished walls. There was an exercise bar along one wall and a large mirror at the front of the room where you could watch yourself do exercises. It was the best room in the whole school, and dance was Connie's favorite class. When she put on her stretchy blue leotard, she felt like a different person; it clung to her thin body and felt less like clothing than like another skin.

"All right, children, sit down." Mrs. Lowry, Connie reflected, seemed to be getting old, her skin was hanging off her throat, people said she was getting ready to retire and that they were getting a new dance teacher. "As you know, children, I am about to retire." Connie resented being addressed as a child. She was, after all, thirteen, and she was serious. "And a new dance teacher, Mrs. Williams, has been selected. Now, Mrs. Williams will be starting with you next week, but she said she'd try to come by this morning and meet all her classes." Mrs. Lowry looked toward the door as if she had delivered a cue, and a moment later, miraculously, the door opened, and Connie's heart simply exploded. The woman was a good head taller than Mrs. Lowry, and every line of her body was dance.

Her hair was short, black, crisply curled, she wore glasses, and her skin was dark. It was the way she walked into the room that shook Connie to her roots; there was almost nothing about her that Connie could associate with ordinary human beings. She walked as if she had descended briefly from some cloud; her legs were long and she made walking look like dancing. She wore a black leotard and a red felt skirt that had sequins embroidered in swirls all over it, and Connie suddenly passionately wished that her leotard were black instead of blue.

"I'm sorry if I'm late, Mrs. Lowry," she said, and her voice charged the air around it, fresh and clean and like some other form of dance. "But they were showing me around the school."

"Perfectly all right. Now, these are the children." Mrs. Williams smiled, and Connie felt her denial of their status as children and moved in closer to catch some of the warmth of that smile. . . . Their new dance teacher was perfect, Connie thought, absolutely perfect. . . .

Then Mrs. Williams began talking, suddenly serious. "I'm going to work you very hard," she said. "Dance is good discipline for you, for your bodies and for your souls. If you aren't serious about dance, then I don't want you here. You should take basketball if you don't want to dance. I want all *my* girls to want to dance." *Her girls.* Connie wanted desperately to be part of that group. "How many of you want to be dancers, professionally, I mean?" Connie's hand shot up, a few other more reluctant ones followed. Mrs. Williams looked at her, and she felt wholly taken in by that look. "What's your name?"

"Connie Bartlett."

"Well, Connie Bartlett, I will expect you to be extremely serious and to lead the others, all right?" Connie nodded her head; it was certainly all right.

In the weeks that followed, she lived totally in relation to her dance class. She was the first there and the last to leave, and she began practicing at home. Watching Mrs. Williams dance was like watching a bird soar; she turned, the red felt skirt swung out and her body sang. She walked in with her drum, no more Mrs. Watson and the piano, and the class began on the beat after her arrival. There was no getting into it, it was just suddenly there, a total atmosphere, and you geared yourself to it, or you lost it. Connie walked around school imitating Mrs. Wanda Williams' walk, trying to look as if she too were about to take off into space, and sometimes she was bad just so that Mrs. Williams would keep her after class and she would have a moment alone with her.

"Connie, I don't know what to do with you. You could be the best dancer here, and sometimes it seems like all you want to do is giggle and play around. I ought to take this," the chamois tipped drumstick, "and beat you like you were the drum." And Connie would promise to be good and would be for a while, until she felt the need come up again to be alone with Mrs. Williams, and then she would be bad. Wanda Williams. Connie walked up and down the halls of the school saying her name over and over again.

She was determined to be a dancer, and then, after the year was up, Mrs. Williams left the school in order to dance with a City Center group, and some of Connie's determination left with her. The next dance teacher was a tiny, pale white woman who seemed to be perenially depressed and could not drag her heavy spirit even two inches off the floor. It was as if a door banged shut on one of the most brilliant worlds that Connie had ever encountered.

The recreation center was noisy; a group of people were playing pool in the back room and four men sat in the front room playing cards. Small children ran back and forth, and the record player blared out "Reach Out to Me." She spoke briefly with the director, and then she went into the bathroom and changed into her leotard and tights. When she came out, she went back into the office and stood talking to the director again. It was after seven, and none of the girls had showed up. In a moment, the door opened, and three girls walked in; the one who was obviously the oldest came up to her.

"Are you Mrs. Wilder? I'm Jane Duval. We're here for dance class."

"Yes," she said, "just call me Connie." Jane nodded and

introduced her to the other two girls: Susie Demps, small and light-skinned, and LaVern Richards, slightly taller, darker, more intense, with eyes that dominated her face.

"LaVern just loves to dance," Susie told her as she disappeared into the bathroom.

"I can see," Connie said. She went back and conferred with the director. It was getting on toward seven-thirty.

"I can clear the front room for you," he said.

"It hardly seems worth it for three girls." She looked around the room. There were five or six girls among the children playing, all of them younger than the three in the bathroom. She went and asked each of them if they wanted to join, and within five minutes she had her first dance class.

They sat in rows facing her, their heads bent over their feet.

"Bounce, two, three, four; Susie, push yourself, you can go farther," and she walked among them, pushing their heads down, straightening legs, from exercise to exercise. She did many of the exercises herself, and the whole thing acquired an intensity that took it outside of time . . . now the Center was quiet . . . they had pulled a corrugated sliding door across the entrance to the poolroom, and the noise was muted. Everyone who was not in the dance class had left, and the coldness of the concrete floor pushed them to exercise harder.

Then across the floor, combinations, prancing, and then leaps, and one of the girls whom Connie had recruited from the floor, a small girl in frayed denim shorts and a faded T-shirt, did magnificent high leaps; she was like a small, awkward gazelle, but all the promise of pure grace and precision was there. And then finally, as the class ended, she had them come and sit in a group around her so that she could get their names and make plans for future classes. Susie sat there poking LaVern, and LaVern kept telling her to stop it.

"What's the matter?" Connie asked.

"LaVern has a dance to do now," Susie said, "but she's shy."

"Would you like to do a dance?" Connie asked her; she didn't want to push anyone too much; there would be time to train them for performing. But LaVern got up and gave her record to the director.

"It's called 'Exodus,' " Susie said to Connie, "and it's real good."

Connie nodded.

The first strains . . . LaVern started her dance with her back to them, one arm raised, her hand clenched in a fist. LaVern danced, and the music pounded in Connie's blood, and every gesture that was part of the dance had that power that she had first seen when LaVern walked in the door. The dance emanated from the very wellsprings of dance; it was pure and whole and said exactly what it had to say; she could scarcely believe that it was being done by a girl who was only fifteen. At the end of the dance, they all clapped, and Connie's eyes filled with tears.

And that was how dance class started.

CHAPTER 7

Summer ripened into pure, almost unendurable heat, and through it all, they danced. She would leave the Center dripping with sweat and drive the girls home feeling a high as original and purely artistic as any she had ever felt. Then she would sit at home long after Alan went to bed, smoking cigarettes in the living room and playing songs on her guitar from so far in her past that she almost felt as if she had met up with a self whom she hardly remembered, the Connie Bartlett of high school and college; curled up on a couch, in her soaking leotard and tights with her old, long ponytail hanging over one shoulder, reaching below her breast....

"Connie, when are you coming to bed?" his voice from the bedroom, at that moment, it might have been her mother's, the tie that binds . . . she was in the clouds. . . .

"Never, probably, at least not tonight . . ." and he would no doubt be looking reproachful, but he must know, at another level, that she was herself again, the Berkeley–New York self that he had always found elusive but that he knew was her happy self, and so he didn't push her.

Or sometimes she would ask him: "Why is it so necessary to you that I go to bed when you do?"

"I just prefer it, that's all."

"But when you're studying, you don't make *me* stay up."

"No, because you're tired and you need to go to sleep."

"So, you need your sleep too, and there's no earthly reason why you should stay awake and listen to me practice guitar."

"I know," but he wasn't convinced, and she didn't feel somehow that she had the right to say to him: Go to bed, I don't want you up while I practice my guitar, this is my world. For, while he tolerated art, he had no understanding of it, and since she had started dance class, she had recognized for perhaps the fifteenth time in her life that art was literally more important to her than food.

And so it went. As they got closer to their first performance, they practiced Saturday afternoons as well as one night a week, and she could feel the tension in the little girls, in LaVern's small cousin, Jeannelle, who was only nine and who had been dragged to dance class by LaVern, who'd thought the class was

45

too small. LaVern and Susie and Jane were the oldest girls in the class, and they dominated it by their skill, their determination and, Connie had to admit, by their tyranny. When she picked up Susie Demps, there might be three small girls in the front seat, scrubbed and proudly wearing their new leotards, but when Susie got in, they had to climb out and sit in the back so that Susie could sit in the front with Connie. Connie hadn't worked that kind of thing out yet, but she knew she would have to; as they did exercises, she tried to get the older ones to help the little ones but not to push them, and after one particularly bad rehearsal, she sat them all down on the floor and talked seriously to them about what they were doing.

"We are the Center Dance Group," she said, "and my name is Connie Wilder, in case you've forgotten. Nobody pays us to be a dance group, nobody pays me to teach you. We are all here because we want to be; anybody who does not want to be here should go home and watch TV, and I'm thinking of putting some of you out." Shades of Wanda Williams . . . "Now there are certain things that we absolutely are, and nobody is going to change those things. We are a group; we are a group as solidly as anyone of us is a person, and nobody is going to mess with that group thing that we are, nobody from outside the group and nobody from inside the group. I do not care what you feel about certain people; that will not come into this group. I don't care who you are used to associating with; while you are in this group, you will associate with all members of this group and treat everybody well, or you will not dance with me. And you will not be nasty or mean to anyone in this group because she is younger than you are. Is that understood?" They would nod their heads and work harder for a while.

Sometimes somebody who really liked coming would stop coming for no apparent reason; then she would have to go round to their house to discuss it; usually she found that they'd dropped out almost accidentally and hardly noticed the act themselves, but that they really wanted to come back. Verena traced it for her to the fact that black people in the South had been forced to do so much that even the children, given a choice of doing something or not, would sometimes just not do it for the hell of it. So she learned something of patience and kept going back to pick up her stragglers. And there was the problem of transportation. Sometimes she would have ten or fifteen kids packed into her '57 Ford because she couldn't get anyone else to drive, but certain things became ritual, and eventually Susie Demps learned to sit in the back seat.

In August, they gave their first performance; the most complex group dance they did was "Very Last Day," and as she stood in the wings and watched them, her eyes filled with tears, and she thought: This world, this awful Orangedale, Florida world is a perfectly incredible place.

And the climax of the dance concert was "Exodus." Most of the audience had heard of LaVern before she went out on stage.

"Oh LaVern, she dance good, she always dance good," and Connie watched her to see if she'd changed, to see if she'd taught her anything, if LaVern needed to be taught anything. It was like watching a fountain rise from the earth; it was one of the purest forms of anything artistic that she had ever seen anywhere, nascent, but rising in an arc, distress, pain, agony, joy and unity with her people and the strength that came artistically when you knew exactly what you had to express and exactly how to express it. Connie found herself in the strange position of knowing that she was the dance teacher of someone who had all the grace and determination to become a great dancer, and she herself was relatively untrained. It was a heady responsibility; she hardly knew what to do with it.

Afterward she and Alan gave a party to celebrate, and she gave each of the girls a chain to wear around her neck, with a glass drop on it containing an opalescent substance floating in water, somehow appropriate. They ate cake and drank punch until it was late for the younger children, and Willie acted very grown-up, and Robin clung to Jeannelle's hand like she would die if she lost it, and the little red-haired girl came over from across the street, crashed the party and told Connie in the kitchen that she had never had any black people in her house except for her maid, and Connie said, "Well, that's too bad."

"Yes." The little girl nodded. "I think it is. Could I have another piece of cake, Mrs. Wilder?" Connie nodded and cut her one.

Late that night, after Alan had taken the girls home and the children were in bed, they sat having a drink in the living room, and he turned to her suddenly and said, "You know, you're a very remarkable woman, and I'm extremely glad I married you," and she kissed him then, slowly, and they went to bed and made love for a long time.

CHAPTER 8

She was sitting on the porch swing, keeping herself rocking by pushing one foot against the floor. It was still August, and the heat had a voice all its own. Their landlady, who lived next door, kept inviting her to come over and "set," all through the heat of last summer and now again, but less this summer because of the numbers of black kids who trooped in and out of her house. Old Southern lady. Old. White. But Connie Wilder didn't generally set, and she didn't know how to explain that to the lady. Sally Krause's voice: Don't let the South get into your bones, Connie. So she wasn't. Dance class apart. Maybe dance class wasn't Southern after all. Maybe, maybe, maybe. She felt her worlds collide, often, her visions of what was and wasn't. . . . She'd never been anywhere like the South, and she wanted now to bring to it something of herself, her Northern New York–Berkeley self, dance class and politics; she didn't want any of it to rub off on her so that when she left, she'd have to take it with her. Her single, primary goal was still to leave. The forces of hatred were everywhere here, tension hanging in the air, atmospheres so thick they seemed to have substance. Rebellion was a steel shaft entering a dead sponge making a clean incision . . . but it came too rarely. Picketing, doing voter registration, drops in the bucket. How she missed the bang and whirl of the city.

The man was coming down the street. He was tall and slender but stooped, and he shuffled as he walked. His face was a dark, mahogany color, soft, beaten, his eyes looking straight ahead, unseeing. She spoke to him every time he went by, and sometimes he spoke to her. The rest of the time he didn't seem to hear her. He always spoke to the children, if they were out front, with infinite gentleness. To her, he said only "Yes, ma'am" or "Thass right, ma'am." She was a white woman and, as such, did not exist except as a force to be placated or avoided. He worked for her landlady next door cleaning up the yard. He worked slowly, more slowly than the landlady herself, and the heat accelerated his slowness. It was all part of the immense, parasitic growth that was the South; green plants grew into one another, flowers grew out of trees, and the

Spanish moss hung down and clung to everything it touched.

"Nice day," she yelled at him so that he couldn't fail to hear her.

"Yes, ma'am." He didn't even look at her. She was thirty-two. He must be seventy. She sighed, and the sigh shook her whole body.

The phone rang, her nerves jumped, and she went to answer it. There was a vast emptiness about her house, even while the children played in it, a loneliness she couldn't control, and the phone was like a sudden signal to life.

She put her hand around the receiver as if she touched flesh. "Hello."

"Hey, Connie, this Alice," a voice like warm water flooding the phone. "You busy tonight?"

"No."

"Me an Van-essa Franklin wants to go out in the country tonight an leave off some voting stuff, and Van-essa's car all tore up. Could you carry us out there?"

"Sure. I'd love to," her feelings not able, she knew, to be matched by her voice, something white people couldn't do.

"See you then. Jes come on when you get through eating." One more thing to do, one more involvement. The way to come South was to come for the Civil Rights Movement, to plan to work twenty-four hours a day; for, except for dance class, all her good moments in the South were connected with civil rights: voter registration, the Black League, the Freedom through Action group, any group that opposed the people she despised, her anger curling and riding her throat. . . .

That night, she drove to Alice's and stopped close to the porch of Alice's shack, a high, gray, weathered porch, three rooms in the shack, creaking, cold in winter, stuffy in summer—six people lived there. Alice came down the steps and got into the car. The sound of tires on a dirt road.

"Hardly got away," Alice said.

"How come?" Connie asked, though it had been true of her too.

"Kids. An' my old man talk like he doin' something I got to stay in for."

"I know that road," Connie said, and they laughed. Alan felt she was doing too much, and she felt she was just beginning to work, just at the edge of where she belonged.

Vanessa's house was large, gray, weathered; the bottom floor had housed a store, but now all that was left of it was a gray empty space behind a window that had "Franklin's" written across it in silver letters that were beginning to flake off at the edges. Next to the window stood a small stone block that enabled you to climb up to the door and ring the bell.

Up the narrow wooden stairs, into Vanessa's living room, with an emphasis on the living. Vanessa stood in the adjoining kitchen cutting the ends off the long stems of the red and white carnations she was arranging in a blue vase, a warm image, the flowers, Vanessa's bright skin and red hair, and the smell of the food they'd had for dinner: pork, sweet potatoes, corn bread.

Vanessa went downstairs with her.

"I gotta stop by T. C.'s," Alice said when they got into the car, "before we go out in the country. Gotta leave stuff off to his place."

"Where's T. C.'s?" Connie asked.

"T. C.'s?" Alice said. "You ain't never been to T. C.'s?"

"I know T. C.," Connie said, "but I've never been to his place. I've hardly been anywhere." It made her feel gloomy.

Vanessa laughed. "Listen to that child. Connie, you really something."

"Turn left at the dirt road," Alice directed.

T. C. Moran. He came to meetings in unpainted churches, and he wore an oversized overcoat and sat in the preacher's corner. He didn't talk much, and sometimes his body fell forward in sleep. People talked a lot about where T. C. lived, and some people said that he had no home at all, and it was legend that he did his sleeping at meetings. Sometimes he brought his niece with him; she was beautiful and had eyes like flowers; her mother was Fontana McClure.

"What's T. C.'s *place?*" Connie asked. "Where he works?"

"Repair shop," Alice said.

"But he doesn't live there?" testing her knowledge.

"No one know where T. C. live."

"He's gotta lotta women he stays with." Vanessa smiled. Connie watched her, wondering. . . .

"That T. C. is a mess," Alice said. "There his place on the left."

It was a wooden shed with a lean-to attached and an aluminum roof covering the whole. A cement floor was scattered with broken car seats, as if it were a living room, and thickly greased parts of cars lay on the floor. And etched out by the moonlight were the half-wrecked bodies of ancient cars in the yard around the lean-to. T. C. came out of the shed onto the steps. He was wearing his work clothes, gray pants and a gray shirt with the sleeves rolled up and half the buttons gone. He came down to greet them:

"Hey, how y'all doin'?" and he smiled, and his face was so open that Connie felt hers open too. . . . "Hey there, Miz Wilder," as if she deserved a special greeting for having arrived there.

"Hi." His "hey" went riding on the night air, and her "hi" rang flat:

"Hey there, Reveren' Moran, what you been up to?"

"Not a thing, just workin'," with his hands lifted in a gesture of innocence.

"I'm not about to believe that." Alice handed him a stack of fliers. "Here're the fliers. Can you take them around to the churches?"

"Sure can, young lady. Where're you ladies bound for now?"

"The country. We're going to put up posters."

He nodded his approbation, smiled, and Connie felt blessed. She wished she could stay.

"Let's go," Alice said. "We stay here talkin' to Reveren' Moran, we won't get nothing done."

He shrugged his shoulders. "All right, but y'all come down to the bus station an' drink some coffee with me one night and we'll plan something. An' come down here for lunch, that's when peoples is here."

They drove off into the lucid darkness, Vanessa and Alice talking and laughing and Connie wound into her own thoughts.

"Picketing Saturday," Alice was saying. "OEO people comin' in to question the state employment people and we picketin' the employment people."

"Nobody I know's gotten a job there."

"You going, Connie?"

"When?"

"Saturday."

"Yes. Definitely."

They drove into a settlement where there was a lighted church and went into the church, and she stood at the back while the voices rose, and the hands clapped, and her heart swelled inside her.

"Holiness church," Alice said to her when they were back outside.

"I liked it," Connie said, knowing Alice's attitude toward it.

"You're a funny girl." Vanessa looked at her appraisingly. "Better come to my church one day. Reveren' Williams, he doesn't take to that holiness stuff. He tries to keep people quieted down."

"Them holiness people near about crazy," Alice said.

"Mm," Connie said, "what's Reverend Moran's church like?"

"T. C. *have* a church now?" Vanessa looked at Alice.

"Two. Somewhere way out in the country. 'Magine he have some wild goings on out there."

"I'd like to go," Connie said.

Vanessa looked at her. "You'd better go to my church," she said firmly.

"What kind of church?" Connie asked her without interest.

"Baptist," Vanessa said. "Reveren' Williams is one of the best preachers we got."

"Okay," Connie said. There was T. C.'s place and the promise of T. C.'s church; there were holiness churches lighting the countryside like occasional flares. Why would she want to go to a Baptist church?

"Well, see y'all later," Alice said when she got out of the car that night. "Don't forget Saturday."

"No," Connie said, "I won't. Picketing at City Hall. I'll be there." And she drove off, back through the tunnel, into a kind of final darkness, with the hymn from the holiness church rocking her.

PART TWO

THE SETTING
OF A PATTERN

He had preached five sermons in two days, two at funerals on Saturday and three on Sunday. Mondays were always bad days. He sat in the church office now, looking out the window at the highway and reflecting on the week ahead. He had committed himself to too much; he knew that already, and if he sat here for more than a few minutes and didn't take the phone off the hook, it would begin ringing. He nourished them on Sundays, and they were back on Mondays for solace. They never really let him go, not even for an hour.

He could feel their need rising in the church. From where he stood, preaching or reading scripture or praying, their need was almost as tangible as thick smoke, and when he blessed them and raised his arms above his head, he prayed silently: Dear God, give me the strength to bear their burdens, for their burdens are so great that I can feel them on my shoulders and taste them in my mouth, and I am not strong enough. And whenever he prayed that, he could feel a force flow into his body, but he knew that the price of that extra strength was that he must in turn increase his efforts to take care of all those people. The intensity of his closeness to that flooding spirit, which he chose to interpret to his congregation as God, was what sustained him. He knew how much more complex it all was than he led them to believe, but he also knew that he gave them just as much of it as they could stand.

He sighed and looked back out the window at the trucks passing and felt a sudden irrational urge to be driving one of them; he could almost feel what the force of it would be like as you drove it along, the crash of it forward as you pressed down on the accelerator and the accompanying sensations of freedom; that was the key to it. He would be driving for days, and no one would know where he was, no one would be able to reach him or make any demands on him. The anonymity and pure pleasure of being alone on the open road. Anything could happen to him there, anything. Here his actions and almost, it seemed to him, his thoughts were monitored by as zealous a bunch of women as God had ever put on this green earth. What could possibly happen to him here? When he had accepted the pastorship of this particular church, he had sworn a verbal oath to do nothing that they would find questionable, and they found almost everything questionable.

He locked the door of his office and walked slowly out to his car. It was a hot, hot summer, and walking quickly in the heat, in the long run, diminished your energy. It was now after one, and if Mozelle preferred him to return for dinner earlier, she had grown accustomed to feeding him whenever he came. There was, as she always said, simply no other way to live with him, and one of the advantages of being married as long as they had been was that once certain patterns were established, they were almost impossible to break, because they were of such long duration. There were conversations between him and Mozelle that were so familiar to him that he had no need to listen to them; he knew his cues, and he could repeat his lines without thinking of them, and so he was perfectly free to think of other things while they talked, without even slightly offending her. He sometimes felt that Mozelle liked to talk mostly to herself anyway.

In his car, he was in his own world. He solved a lot of the problems other people brought to him while he was driving; he liked the car's sleekness and power, and he thought of it more as an animal than as a machine, and as an asset. When the car was washed and waxed and he was dressed up, whether for church or to go downtown, together they created an image. For *his* people, it was an image of leadership and security, even of aristocracy; for the white people downtown, it was an image of the power of a black man. And if the validity of that image was ever called into question, there was always the gun in the glove compartment.

He pulled into the driveway, took the mail out of the box and started up the porch steps; it was always at this precise moment that the dilapidated condition of his own home caught his eye and momentarily held his attention. I must work on the house, he thought, but his time was siphoned away by other people's problems, and his money found its way into other people's pockets, and so the house never got repaired.

"Hey, Revren' Williams," the man across the road called to him from his porch.

"Hey there, Mr. Crockett, how you doing?"

"Oh, I'll make it, I guess, but my arthuritus got me down."

"That's a shame, Mr. Crockett," opening the door.

"Jason?"

"Mm," feeling that he could not afford to waste his energy even on extra words.

"I'm glad you've come. Mrs. Wallace called and said that her roof's leaking, says if there's anymore rain, she's fixin' to drown and wants to know if you'd get her roof straight for her."

"Yes," he said as he sat down and put his glasses on to read the mail, "I can do it tomorrow."

"She doesn't have money."

"I know," he said. "That's why she called me."

"You ready for dinner?"

"Mm hmmm." He read through his mail rapidly while she put the food out on the table: requests for assistance of one sort or another, a couple of bills, the program for a church conference he had to attend. . . .

"Aw right," she said, "come on." He got up slowly and went over to the table. He knew what it was by its familiar smell before he got there: fried chicken and greens and sweet potatoes and corn bread, the fried chicken of thousands of accumulated Sundays, the fried chicken of all the Mondays afterward . . . he had grown to hate fried chicken, but he ate it, commented on all the chickens of all the ladies of his two congregations and listened to their wearisome discussions: "Now some people know how to fry a chicken and some people jes' don't. . . . Now I . . ." And so it went. It was all part and parcel of the demands that were made upon him. He didn't even care about eating. He could not get excited about food, and he went through the eating ritual only whenever he felt his physical strength going or his powers of concentration temporarily diminishing. It was only on Sundays at church dinners that he even feigned real enthusiasm about the piles of food that were in some oblique way related to his calling.

He bowed his head and said grace. He could feel her waiting to say something even during grace. Prayers were spaces in the day where no one could intrude; they bore some relation to the mystic presence of God and nature, those presences that carried him through and made the pain and the noise almost bearable sometimes.

"Now," Mozelle said, "now that we're eating and you're rested . . . " He looked at her before he took his second mouthful of potato—there was no way in the world that she could think he was rested. "I want to say that Sister Green was not in church yesterday, and that's the third Sunday in a row." Her feeling of contempt for Sister Green was evident in her expression. . . .

"Sister Green's all right, Mozelle." He didn't want to discuss it. "She'll be back."

"You oughta tell her she's got to be back; she missed choir rehearsal twice too. Things are not the way they used to be. It used to be that if you missed twice, you weren't allowed to be in the choir."

"Mm hmmm." He was tuning himself out, eating, calculating what he had to do this afternoon. Sometimes he wished he saw things the way she did. Her vision was clear, and her rules were absolute. If you broke one of the rules, you were crazy or sinful, and either way, her job or his, as *she* saw it, was to get the erring person back on the right road. In Sister Green's case, absence from church symbolized other indiscretions: she'd been known to take a drink, "crazy" was Mozelle's interpretation of that, and since Sister Green had been widowed, she'd been known to take a man into her bedroom, "sinful under the sight of the Lord."

He finished his meal and rose. "I'll think about Sister Green," he said. "I have a lot of work to do this afternoon and a meeting at five. I don't know what time I'll be back."

"Aw right." She was clearing away the dishes. "But you're too easy on these people, Rev, too easy. They need to learn about sin, and they ain't never gonna learn as long as they stay away from church."

"Mm." The door banged. He was already out on the front porch smoking a cigarette, watching how the sun gleamed on a tree across the road and made the leaves stand out bright and stiff. Easy. He found nothing easy, and each time he made any kind of judgment, he had to know enough . . . and to put himself inside a person's life. Sister Green was a good woman; he knew that but simply could not say it to Mozelle, for she had no ears to hear it. Sometimes he would look across at her and wonder how they had ever married and founded generations together when they saw almost nothing in the same way. He crushed his cigarette out under his foot; staring at the tree across the road, he thought again of being a truckdriver. He needed something, for, despite the way he trained his mind to penetrate the most abstruse theological and philosophical works he could find, which was his way of keeping his mind honed, he felt something deep within himself going stale.

PART THREE

THE TAMING
OF CONNIE WILDER

Saturday . . . and still the August heat, hanging in the air, with the humidity like a felt pressure on her head. There was a group of people already gathered on the plaza outside City Hall when Connie got there: people from the Black League, from FTA and bunches of students. She stood talking to LaVern and Susie, who had been recruited through their high-school group, and she felt proud of them and protective; they seemed young for civil-rights stuff.

"Hey, Connie." Ward Miles came over and handed her a sign. He was the president of the FTA and organized most of the picketing. "This one okay?" The sign said: "Give the Job to the Smartest Man, Black or White."

"Yeah, that's fine." She hooked the wire hanger over her head and adjusted the sign so that the top of it came just under her shoulders. You had to be careful or the picket sign slipped, and then it kept banging you as you walked, just at the level of your nipples. Dignity at all costs. She got on the line and watched Ward, who stood talking to several women who were mixing a big tub of punch for the picketers. Ward was smart and direct and energetic. He was the kind of man you'd consider having an affair with, she thought, if you were considering having an affair. Which she wasn't. There were currencies in the movement, and one of the currencies was that the only free people in the South were the black woman and the white man who slept together.

"That's where it's at, brother, they free," a square-built dark man shouting in a church at some meeting, and at the end, they'd held crossed hands and sung "We Shall Overcome" with that proud feeling of unity they possessed, and the dark man next to her had squeezed her hand tightly.

The speaker, with his talk of sex, had laced the minds of the group around that topic, so when several couples went out to drink later, they talked about the students in the movement and whether they'd gone the "sexual route." Connie had sat listening, wondering; traditionally it had been the white man and the black woman who had slept together rather than the white woman and the black man, because the white man had had the power to do what he wanted; the speaker had called them free, but if the black woman had been coerced, then how could they be? . . . The black man and the white woman who slept together, on the other hand, would be free because they would both be choosing to, but, despite the loose talk about the students, she was convinced that this couldn't happen in the South. She'd never heard of its happening.

She greeted people on the picket line. Whatever the currencies of the movement, whatever its exaggerations and occasional falseness, there was a feeling of community all through it, particularly on the picket line. She was in a clear, good mood, something happening inside her related to the community around her. She was at total peace with herself.

"Hey, Connie, how you doin'?" Alice stepped into line in front of her.

"Hi, Alice."

They talked, and slowly the rhythm of walking began to guide her. The sun was hot enough so that she could feel her dress wet against her back, soaking, and the sweat pouring down between her breasts; living in Florida, drenched in sweat, she was almost becoming used to it, heat falling and filling the air. And then the people began arriving at the meeting. The people from OEO looked like knights from a distant land, tall, straight, intelligent, purposeful, while the people from the State Employment Office looked pale, some of them fading into a frightening kind of whiteness, others with hard, ruddy faces, all of them with blank, unseeing eyes. A few black people were going into the hearing too, teachers or preachers, social workers, people with an interest in getting people jobs, and while they weren't all beautiful, they all had dignity.

"Hey, Connie, don't you want something to drink?" Vanessa.

"Keep in line," Ward ordered. "Don't keep messing up the lines. Stay at least two feet from each other, and don't drop off. The line doesn't look like anything."

Vanessa brought cups of punch to the line, and people drank while they walked.

She became acutely conscious of the sun, suddenly, as if it held her in some trancelike state, and the heat became more intense the longer she walked. A tall slender, blond girl got on the line, a girl with her white skin dappled by veins; there were dark girls whose skin glowed in the sunlight, and the visual impact of the whole was immense. At the point when she was thinking that she'd really like to rest, a couple of cars pulled up, and a reporter and photographer got out and snapped pictures and asked questions; she felt her spirits rise, as if by being photographed and written up their act had attained a new dimension. The walking carried them, created the performance of their feeling so that the audience could watch. And the heat gave to the performance an atmosphere that caught and held her, and when somebody yelled at her that it was lunchtime, she barely heard and kept on walking.

And so she was on the picket line when he came out of City Hall and she saw him. A light exploded in her head and filled her and burst forth. He was tall, and he stood so that she saw his profile, dark, smoky features, a brooding expression on his face, his eyelids lowered slightly. His dignity struck her like a shaft to the heart.

Other people came out then behind him, and he began talking with them. They stood, they talked and the whole had an aura of significance, as if affairs of state were settled in his circle. The light slowly faded inward.

"That's the most beautiful man I've ever seen," she said to Alice. "Who is he?"

"Which one?"

Connie pointed.

"Oh, that's Reveren' Williams, Vanessa's pastor."

"Oh." Reverend. Vanessa's pastor. Baptist, those who dripped holy water on children's heads. Foolish. Still the beauty remained. And shook her.

"Break the lines, everyone, break for lunch," Ward's voice, domineering, and they obediently trailed over to the tub of punch, where some of the women were giving out sandwiches. She sat on the grass eating a peanut-butter sandwich and watching Reverend Williams. He turned to face their group, the sun on his face; his skin was the color of wood stained chestnut, like redwood, a rich Indian color. A moment before, it had seemed darker, the darkest of browns, and in his face were the two cultures: African and Indian. He was still talking, yet there was an air of absence in the way he talked, as if there was a part of him that he held in reserve. He spoke, his eyes took in the group she was with, passed over her, and she turned to listen to something Ward was saying:

"When I was in there, this man from the employment office got up and contradicted himself three times. Man, I knew they were stupid, but I never expected this kind of crawfishin'."

She took in Ward's words, but the man on the steps drew her, the power of those eyes—dark and somehow kindled. She lit a cigarette. "Ward, you got enough people for this afternoon?"

He smiled. "You wanta see the fireworks inside, huh?"

"Yeah, I'd like to. This is the most that's happened since I've been here." He laughed and got up from the grass in one smooth motion. African motion. Racist myths. She saw it in dance class every week and knew. It wasn't just rhythm, it was much more. The black kids moved like liquid, one motion where the white kids needed six.

"Back to the line, everyone." Ward clapped his hands. People rose from the grass, broke up the groups in which they'd been standing and talking, and jumped down from the hoods of cars. They crushed their cigarettes out on the plaza and picked up their signs.

Inside City Hall it was cool, with the coolness dropping from the ceiling and easing out of the walls, and the air conditioning washed over her, caressing her skin. She opened the back door of the meeting room. At the front were long tables where the OEO people and the newspaper reporters were sitting. In front of them was a small table and chair, where the person testifying sat. She went in quietly and stood against the back wall.

"Is it true that this firm employed more than one hundred persons?" the lawyer was asking.

"Well, suh, ah cain't rightly say. There're a lot of things that don't go on our forms always."

"Well, did this go on your forms?"

"Oardinarily, it would have, but in this case, it hadn't been put there."

"And you didn't send it back to have it corrected?"

"No."

"Don't you think that was a little careless, since people's jobs were at stake?"

"Ah suppose by yoah standards it was."

She turned, looking for one of her friends so that she might communicate her disbelief, and there he was, smiling at her, ironic, detached from what was happening, making her feel that it existed only that they might communicate about it. He laughed then, a slight laugh, way down in his throat, and she became suddenly conscious of her uncombed hair and her wet dress, conscious with a sensation that invaded every nerve of her body.

When he left the room, she waited a full minute and followed him. Absurd to do this, she told herself. She closed the door behind her, and there he was, sitting in a chair, smoking. Imperturbable. Something aristocratic about him. An African king.

"Atmosphere too thick for you too?"

"Yes." She took out a cigarette, trying to cultivate at least a small circle of imperturbability to match his. He got up to light the cigarette for her. "You going to march to the courthouse with us?" she asked.

He laughed, a rough, deep laugh, rough like his voice. "No, I'm too old to go in for any of that foolishness." She shrugged her shoulders, feeling an awkwardness settle between them. Her eyes went to his face, searching for the meaning of the remark, but she could detect nothing. "I might meet you down there," he said.

"Good." She smiled. "Well, I guess I'd better go back and picket. That's what I'm supposed to be good for."

"Don't go out there again. You'll get yourself sick in all that sun."

"I'm an extremist."

He put out his cigarette. "C'mon." He gestured. "Let's go back in and see what the fool's sayin' now." And she found herself following, obeying him without question, going back into the meeting room and sitting down when he gestured her to a seat.

Late in the afternoon, when the hearing was all over, they assembled outside, and fifty of them marched double file the twenty blocks to the courthouse. The heat turned to rain; her hair got wet and was plastered against her back as they walked: now on sidewalks, now through the mud, turning their signs toward the endless cars that passed along the street, many of them with confederate license plates, as the people drove home from work. People jeered, hooted and honked, but they read the signs, and the spirit on the line ran high. They told jokes, and they sang freedom songs.

When they reached the courthouse, they sat in front of it, and they sang again, and then Reverend Williams emerged from nowhere and raised his arms in a gesture of blessing while they all bowed their heads, and T. C. was there. And they all prayed and sang, and there was a flood of feeling within her. Here in front of the courthouse, with the rain easing off and the first rays of the late afternoon sun shining, here, with Reverend Williams blessing them and a song pressing somewhere inside her, here was where she belonged.

CHAPTER 11

The last few weeks of an impossibly hot summer . . . voices across a hot street, a man fixing his motorcycle, the clarity of sound cutting into the atmosphere, her ponytail wet down her back until she looped it into a knot and stuck it full of hairpins . . . sitting on her porch swing, pushing herself back and forth with her foot, she watched a speckled butterfly opening and closing its wings, opening and closing . . . and beyond, the bright green of the palms . . . the screen pressed a pattern into the sky . . . ; if you looked at palm fronds upside down, they were like sabers, green steel rain; the butterfly remained on the screen for a moment, opening and closing its wings, hesitating, poised for its flight, but seeming almost miraculously glued to the screen as if for a final moment of reassurance before . . . freedom . . . ; she could almost feel the pull, the tension in its wings, her own irresolution. . . . She hadn't seen Reverend Williams since the hearings, and she found herself thinking about him only on the deeper levels of her mind, those almost unreachable passages of thought where unseen images floated . . . the flash of a single rocket, lightning breaking a black surface, one's life substantially unaltered by the passion of moments.

At the tail end of the summer, Sally Krause came back, and Connie drove her around to see the sights: Silver Springs, Marineland, the McKee Jungle Gardens, lush heavy tropical sights with orange juice spouting from the palm trees and endless tourists milling in and out . . . the kids loved it, she felt remote. With Sally, she talked civil rights and the movement (the student term for it all, involving at that point in history the war in Vietnam and, somewhat obscurely, sex and four letter words), and Sally looked bemused and told her she had swamp fever after all. So be it.

"Now the real world . . . ," she said to Sally one day while they were doing dishes.

"Connie, the real world is everywhere, the real world is what we're all living in," Sally, with a laugh, drying her soft, white hands on a towel, rubbing off water, soap and the thought of the world's dirt.

"Of course, all of us have known for sometime that you're crazy."

Connie smiled, scooping up a handful of soap bubbles, watching the light slide colored surfaces onto the surfaces of the bubbles. It wasn't an insult or a compliment, it was one order of fact. "You *did* say that you wanted to see the spade scene."

Sally laughed again. "So that's the real world now, is it? I should've guessed. Sure I want to see it."

"We'll go to T. C.'s tomorrow," Connie said, but Sally had taken the edge off her enthusiasm. Being crazy was one thing, but being ridiculed about her deepest convictions was another.

"What's T. C.'s?"

"T. C. Moran's garage."

Sally raised an eyebrow. "Garage?"

"You'll see."

They sat around having after-dinner drinks, she and Alan and Sally; Alan and Sally talked about Van Gogh, and her attention wandered; she wasn't at all sure that any line of communication could be set up between Sally and T. C. And yet that line existed between her and T. C. She knew that she was following, blindly, a path that was going to lead her to places she was totally unfamiliar with. That was almost all she knew except that she was going to discover some options she hadn't known existed and would have to reject some others she had once thought of as assumptions rather than options. It was how you saw things, the nature of your vision. How you saw poverty, that had once been an option for her. She could remember the day in New York when it had ceased to be. . . .

. . . She was standing in the high, lighted vault of Grand Central Station waiting for Yvonne del Gado. The train was already twenty minutes late. Yvonne had been to a private home for the summer; some of the kids went to camp, and some of them went to private homes up through New England all the way to Maine, and some of them went south as far as Virginia. Yvonne had gone to Massachusetts to visit a Mrs.

Wilson, and Connie had to check her in before she went home with her parents.

She slid onto a bench, exhausted by the heat and the endless nights at the stations; it was late August, and the stations were the hottest, most humid places in the whole city.

She took Yvonne's record out of her pocketbook and read it over: Yvonne del Gado, nine years old. The address was on East 100th Street. Her father was an unemployed welder with a petty-theft record. Her mother had tuberculosis. She was one of eight children. Connie could feel the hopelessness of it as a physical sensation, but she could no longer consider a situation like Yvonne's unusual, because it simply wasn't. With certain changes came others. She, Connie Bartlett, in some sense no longer belonged to the world she came from, but she didn't belong to Yvonne del Gado's world either. She was simply a link.

People streamed suddenly out of the dark tunnel from the train, and Connie got up quickly and went over to the entrance to wait. Mrs. Wilson and Yvonne weren't hard to pick out. Mrs. Wilson was tall and slender, suburban-cool-looking. Yvonne had large, brown eyes, neat pigtails and was wearing an obviously new turquoise dress. She was a precise, immaculate, breathtakingly beautiful little girl.

"Mrs. Wilson." Connie went up to her.

"Oh, hello, the train was late. Isn't that a shame? I'm afraid we've kept you waiting. You're Connie Bartlett, aren't you?"

Connie nodded.

"Well, this is Yvonne, and here's a note for her parents." She handed Connie a pale-blue envelope. "And here are her papers and her suitcase. I had planned to take her all the way home, but I have to meet my husband in half an hour. She's a perfectly wonderful child. . . ."

"I'll be glad to take her home," Connie said and was; she saw so many of the kids for only a few minutes. The chance for some kind of relationship, however tenuous, however brief, was always welcome. Mrs. Wilson squatted down and kissed Yvonne.

"Good-bye, darling," she said. "You'll come and see us again next year, won't you?"

Yvonne nodded.

Mrs. Wilson got up quickly. "A wonderful child," she said again, and there were tears in her eyes. "Thank you." She turned and walked away.

"Did you have a good time?" Connie asked Yvonne.

"Yes," her gravity a mask for ...

"How many children does Mrs. Wilson have?"

"Two, Nancy and Cindy." She smiled dreamily. "I slept in Nancy's room. She's nine like me."

They stopped, and Connie switched the suitcase to her other hand. Yvonne stood clutching the handle of her red plastic pocketbook tightly in her hand. They were standing by a hamburger counter cut into the wall of the station.

"Do you want something to eat?" Connie asked her. Yvonne looked up at Connie, assessing her, hesitating for a moment.

"Yes," she said, and they went in and bought a hamburger and a Coke.

They got onto the dirty, rattling subway and sat down. Yvonne held her hamburger carefully away from her dress so that she wouldn't spot it. Connie read an ad on the dangers of venereal disease and tried to think of what to say next.

"What are your brothers' and sisters' names?" she asked finally.

"Carmen, Maria, José, Enriqué, Dolores, Hernando, Luis." Yvonne reeled them off with incredible speed, as if they were the words of a popular song.

"Four boys and four girls," Connie said. "That's nice."

Yvonne shook her head. "It's too many," she said without emotion.

They reached Seventy-second Street, and Connie realized that she was still carrying Yvonne's Coke. "Don't you want your Coke and hamburger now?" she asked. "We're getting off pretty soon."

Yvonne shook her head.

"When are you going to have them."

"At home. I take them home for my brothers and sisters."

74

They reached Ninety-sixth Street.

"Come on," Connie said. "We have to get off." They walked across the blank, dark platform and up the stairs and then toward 100th Street. Tenements lined the streets, high, frail buildings with fire escapes up the front . . . ; it was after five now, but the heat hadn't lifted. They walked along narrow streets, past card games, past the garbage thrown in the gutters, past a drunk, past a dark huddle of boys over a crap game in a dark doorway. Connie steered Yvonne around obstacles, crossing the street whenever the other side looked temporarily more promising, and realizing even as she did so that it was absurd to try and protect Yvonne, because Yvonne lived here, and these were her streets.

One-hundredth Street, and as they walked east, the street seemed to Connie narrower, the houses seemed to grow into the street, the people were crowded out of the houses, down the steps and onto the thin strips of sidewalk. People watched them as they crossed Second Avenue, people watched them enter their world, watched her as an alien force; everything around her was strangely muted; there was no money to make anything distinguishable from anything else. . . .

The men who sat hunched over the game tables too seemed indistinguishable, one from another—white shirts had become soiled, dark suits faded. Girls stood in doorways, young, slender girls and heavier girls whose breasts rose above their necklines; there were girls grinding down the street; it was a world of hustling, the hustlers and the hustled. It was this world that Connie brought Yvonne back to.

"Hullo, Yvonne." A girl Yvonne's age called her from a doorway. Her hair fell in stiff bunches to her shoulders; she wore a torn and dirty dress. Her face was not unlike Yvonne's, thin and delicately boned and pretty.

"Hello," Yvonne called back, detached, still part of her past experience. They walked past Lucille's Beauty Parlor, past the Ideal Pharmacy, past the dark boys in doorways whose silk shirts were tucked loosely into tight pants.

"Here's my house," Yvonne said.

"Where?" Connie asked.

"Here." She pointed at a gaping black hole. Above it stretched an apartment building, but the entrance was simply blackness. When Connie's eyes had become accustomed to the darkness, she saw a shaky stairway in the depths of the entrance. "Thank you," Yvonne said, "I can go alone now," with such dignity and sensitivity, as she felt their worlds parting.

"Can you carry everything?"

She nodded and took the Coke and the suitcase from Connie.

"Okay," Connie said. "Good-bye. Don't forget to give Mrs. Wilson's letter to your mother," as if a letter in a pale-blue envelope could have any meaning . . . but maybe . . .

"I won't. Good-bye." She smiled. Then she turned and went in. Connie stood watching her move away, a small, strong figure, the bright blue a single spot of color in the dark hall. Yvonne became smaller, started up the stairway, and Connie found herself suddenly alone, the flash of blue gone and the sounds of the street roaring in her ears. She heard a long, low whistle from a doorway as she started walking, and realized that, of course, if she had had the illusion that she was protecting Yvonne, Yvonne had also been protecting her. But she didn't feel afraid; it was her city too, and its hazards were her hazards. There was nothing that could have stopped her from doing work that involved what some people might have called danger. She didn't like people to mention danger; she didn't want to hear about it.

Darkness was pouring in now and mingling with the heat. The grotesque, spilled eyes of a junkie stared at her from a doorway. From a doorway, the words themselves haunted her, doorways to nothingness. . . . She crossed Second Avenue again, a lone bus hurtling by her. . . . Reality, it would have to be a path to commitment, so that you never forgot children swallowed by doorways, so that you would use your energy to prevent it from happening over and over again. . . .

. . . That had been the night she'd lost one of her options, the wholly comfortable middle-class option of treating the poor as if they did not exist, of treating them as an abstraction.

"Connie, where are you?" Sally.

"Mm, oh nowhere, just thinking."

"My wife is a guitar-playing, dancing dreamer. Her world is somewhere so far off that I only manage to catch glimpses of it when it passes by sometimes." He and Sally were laughing.

"Connie used to drive her teachers crazy. I remember the math instructor. Connie was always into something, and one day Miss Bristol just lost her composure completely and said, 'Connie, can't you ever do anything the way other people do.' I think that was the day Connie handed her math in with flowers all the way around the border." Sally told the story, and Alan laughed happily.

"Well, it *looked* nice." She was exasperated. "Why on earth shouldn't you hand in your math homework with flowers on it?"

"Just because." Alan spoke to her sometimes as if she were a child. "People don't do it that way." He and Sally laughed again, companionably, and Connie fell into a sullen silence, looking around at their house, a compromise between what he'd wanted, a stone-block modern, definitely middle-class house in a definitely middle-class neighborhood, and what she'd wanted, a large habitable shack in a definitely lower-class neighborhood. He had taken this house, though it was not what he wanted, because "he had wanted to make her happy." It was not really, she knew, that this house made her happy but simply that it made her less unhappy.

"Good night," she said, "I'm going to bed."

"Okay," Alan replied. "As soon as Sally and I kill this bottle, I'll be ready to sleep too."

She kissed him absently and walked off with a vague wave at Sally. For Alan, he was high, and the idea flickered through her mind that he might want to go to bed with Sally, and she wondered if she would care, and strangely enough, for the first time in her life, she felt that she really wouldn't.

The next day, slightly after noon, they drove over to T. C.'s, she, Sally, Willie and Robin. The kids adored T. C.'s and were learning to fix cars. Alan drove a '60 Buick, and she drove a rattletrap Ford and used its breakdowns as an excuse to talk to T. C. Her car had a loose door, a cracked window and a cranky motor. She turned off the road into the yard around the garage. She could see T. C.'s feet emerging from under a car. She stopped, turned off her motor, and the kids got out.

"Hey, T. C., I'll help you." Willie ran over and got down on his stomach so that he could talk to T. C. under the car.

T. C. slid out and got up. "Hey, how y'all doin'?" He took out a large handkerchief and wiped his hands; then he and Connie shook hands, and she introduced him to Sally. "How you doin', Miz Krause?" T. C. smiled, and his face opened. Around them, the sun gleamed on the bodies of cars, on the dented cabs of trucks, on the open curves of fenders.

"Fine, Reverend Moran."

"Brought you some lunch, T. C." Connie opened the bag and took out a Coke and a sandwich.

"Man, I was just fixin' to go get me some lunch. The Lord's gonna bless you, young lady. Let me go wash up." And he went into the shed with Willie behind him. Robin was out at the edge of the yard climbing on a pickup truck.

"Here." Connie dusted a chair off for Sally. Even in slacks, Sally required a certain amount of attention. Connie curled up on a broken car seat and sipped her Coke.

"Well?" she asked Sally.

"Well, what? Jesus." She shook her head. "He only said three words. You really expect miracles."

Connie nodded, knowing the truth of it.

T. C. came out on the steps of the shack then, rubbing his hands on a rag. "That little girl's one of the best civil rights workers we got," he said, and Sally nodded. Even T. C. seemed uncomfortable, and it took a lot of tension to make T. C. uncomfortable. "What's been happenin' lately?" He turned to Connie for the answer.

"Repercussions from the hearing," she said. "The employment service is nervous, but it'll be a long time before anything really concrete gets done." As she spoke, her words seemed to echo doubly, once in the space between her and Sally and once in the space between her and T. C. Sally was waiting for something familiar to happen. But this was T. C.'s. Sally might never encounter another place where things were done in a way so different from her own. The difference lay in speed. T. C. let things unfold more slowly; petal by petal, flowers opened until the sun hit them in their full openness; things of the heart unfolded more slowly than things of the mind. And the difference lay in tone, in quality. What happened at T. C.'s was an atmosphere; it blew full like mist, hung in the air for a moment and then disappeared.

"Well, I hold," T. C. said, "I hold that they'll do something now. Down through the years, the Southern white man has waited till there was national pressure, an' that's what you got now. What we got here is a gradual 'vealin' of the situation which we known to exist since slavery days. It's the catching up of one group with another." Sally was restive; Connie knew she would feel she could get her black education out of James Baldwin. "There're a lot of people who've done a lot of speakin' down the line, like my buddy Revren' Williams, an' we gotta get all the people behind them."

Into her mind's locked combination fell the tumblers—Reverend Williams. Connie had been about to get up; now she sat back and waited.

"How is Reverend Williams these days? I haven't seen him for a while."

"That man so tired. He been runnin' all over the county. He been preachin'. He's the head of all the Baptists in the county, an' he's gotta lot of buildin' jobs this season too."

"Building jobs?" with a polite half-lack of interest.

"He's a carpenter and a builder, builds a lot for people without money."

"That's an appropriate profession for a preacher," Sally from her mounted perch. "Is he a Christlike type?"

T. C. laughed, a single chuckle emerging from deep within him and hitting the air with such force that Connie smiled, but T. C. didn't answer. "That man so tired he gonna' get hisself sick if he ain't careful."

"Then he better be careful, you can tell him for me. He's

too valuable to let himself get sick." Then she got up. "Sally and I have to go downtown for a while. Could we leave Willie and Robin here?"

"Sure." T. C. finished his Coke and gave her the bottle.

"You don't have to say anything," Connie said as they drove off. "These things don't usually work out."

Sally lighted a cigarette. "Now the one I'd like to meet," she said, "is Reverend Williams."

"Why?" A flash went through her.

"He sounds like the last Renaissance man."

"Probably so."

"Tell me what he's like."

"I can't. I hardly know the man."

And later, as they were having drinks before dinner and Sally was scanning the Orangedale *News*: "Well, what do you know, they've appointed your Reverend Williams to the local Human Rights Commission."

"Good. And he's not *my* Reverend Williams. I told you I barely know him." But the light held its own, shafts of it going into her limbs and into her heart. . . .

CHAPTER 12

The courthouse itself was a big stone structure with a stone plaza all around it and fountains rising out of the plaza. Orangedale had only two plazas, a small one at City Hall and a huge one at the courthouse. Patches of grass grew in the cracks between the squares of stone and were trimmed. The corridors of the courthouse rose high, and you felt your dignity increase when you walked along them and heard your footsteps echo off the terrazzo floors; all the doors at the courthouse opened like pushed wind, and the Coke machines gleamed at the end of the corridors.

When Connie entered the courtroom, she knew he was there, because something happened to the room. She sat down in the back. He was sitting right in front of her, so close that she could have reached out and touched the back of his head, and his closeness was a warm liquid washing over her body.

The room was crowded, and the atmosphere was charged with people's feelings. He took out a cigarette, lighted it, and the smoke from his cigarette rose and grew into the general smoke of the room. He smoked almost all the time, and it was almost an accompaniment to what he said:

"We have been discussin' the need for good housing for years. The problem is there. The real issue now is what plan would be most profitable for this community, what government plan. But people keep bringing up the question of whether or not we *need* to clear up the slums, whether they're that bad. Well, they might go and see them if they want to know. I don't think, though, that anyone who doesn't know the condition of the slums is qualified to speak to this body about housing at all." He sat down. Applause. She clapped.

"Nobody would deny"—it was G. M. Swinburne rising from his chair without being called upon—"nobody would deny that they-uh is a great need for good housin' fuh all. Nobody could disagree with Revrun Willyums. Noah would anyone disagree, ah'm sure, about the good intentions of city bodies with regard to providin' this housin' fuh all in the most expedient manner possible. I say most expedient manner possible because we all know that it is *not* possible to have all the things we want done as soon as we would like to have them done. And the methodology is what we are discussin' here, the methodology and inahdvahsability of taking this mattuh out of ow-uh own hands, which is to say the guvment of the lan'. Ah say that ow-uh own guvment, the guvment of the city of Orangedale, Florida can handle this and will handle this, all in due time."

"Shoot, the government of Orangedale, Florida doesn't have half the money to do the job that's needed here," Reverend Williams, without getting up out of his seat.

"Revrun Willyums, ah beg you, suh, to regard the situation for what it is worth. We have the option of sellin' out to this heah guvment pressure, tryin' to cum in an tell us how to run ow-uh city, oah either we have the choice of keepin' this in ow-uh own hands. The awlternative, ah assure you, would be to hand over ow-uh town to the fedrul guvment to do with what they wanted."

"Mister Chairman." Reverend Williams had his hand up again, and he had a way of doing it as if he were complying with the formalities out of courtesy, as if there could be no doubt that in any situation he would be called upon, because his prerogatives were the prerogatives of a king. He stood up. "Mister Chairman, with all due respect to the eloquence of Mr. Swinburne and to his feeling for tradition, there comes a time when things have got to be changed. He objected to my using the simple question of money as a reason for applying to the federal government, so let me change ground. This housin' concerns the poor, an' if you can show me one substantial thing that the government of Orangedale, Florida has done for the poor, ever, I'll be extremely surprised." He sat down to more applause, and the discussion went on while she concentrated on the back of his neck, on the way he lighted his cigarette, on the kind of remark he made to the people near him.

After the meeting, they all went outside the courtroom, stood around smoking and bought Cokes out of the machine.

"Mrs. Wilder?" He handed her one.

"Thank you." She fished in her purse for change.

"It's a gift," his voice different. He had different voices for different occasions.

"Thank you again."

He put his hat on and pushed it back so that he looked like a Mississippi River gambler. Mustache, dark, intense eyes.

Someone said something about the housing situation, and she pulled herself out of her trance. "You've gotta make a big stink," she said. "Picket the Housing Authority and put pressure on them. Pull a rent strike if we can get it organized."

"That's you, always wanting to make a big stink," he said, and she smiled but watched him for what lay beneath the tone of the remark. His eyes went from her face to her breasts and back again. So! Reverend. He, like T. C., was a new kind of person for her, someone she hadn't known existed. Now he looked tired, and she thought of what T. C. had said about how hard he worked.

Downstairs, when they were all going in different directions toward their cars, she felt a wrench. She should have been going with him. The absurdity of the thought struck her almost as quickly. He was, after all, a virtual stranger. It was much later that night that she realized, as she played her guitar and sang, that every man that she'd ever cared about had started off being a stranger. . . .

He'd been in the hospital almost a week when she heard about it. She kept contact with T. C. during the next week, and so she knew exactly when he got out of the hospital. She knew with the knowledge that only T. C.'s ample clinical details could give that he was okay, and she breathed a sigh of relief.

She could feel conflicts telling on her life . . . the pure-American-woman-dream. She, Connie Wilder, had it made. So said the modern version of the dream. Alan was a successful lawyer, and he was going to be even more successful. They had two bright, healthy kids. She had her work, studying literary listory, and seemed good at it, so that as the children matured, she would have what was commonly referred to as a career. She and Alan, liberal-radical-idealists or something,

absorbed in their own brand of politics, useful . . . yet . . .
yet . . . yet . . . The South had told on her and Alan, on the
way they were together, on their nerves, and so she increasingly
found herself looking forward to meetings, to the freedom of
being away from both the house and graduate school. . . .
There was the excitement of learning totally new things, and
now there was the slight added prospect that at any meeting
he might be there. . . .

They sat down to dinner.
"You going out tonight?" Alan looked up from his plate.
"Yes."
"I wish you wouldn't."
"Alan, it's an important meeting on voting rights." She
could feel her will asserting itself, not in her voice, but in
the very marrow of her bones.
"You're doing too much."
"If the few people who're active fink out, the movement
here has had it."
"True." He buttered a roll and sighed. "Very true."
"Anyway . . ." There was a vicious part of her that rose
involuntarily to the surface. She watched it come up within
her now as if it were on film. "*You* don't do it."
"True again." He looked at her with disgust. "But unneces-
sary to say. You know how much work I have to do. I *do* pay
the bills."
"I'm sorry, I mean, I'm really sorry I'm like that."
Willie and Robin eating placidly, or so it seemed. "*What*
are you like, Mommy?" Willie looked up at her with his
glowing brown eyes.
"Awful," but she smiled.
"Her's mad," Robin said, picking up spoonfuls of her apple-
sauce and dropping them back in the dish.
"Maybe," Connie said, "but don't play with your applesauce."
She started clearing off the table.

Night. A single street lamp lighting the dirt road. People
were filing out of the church and gathering on the steps and

the road to talk. She and Vanessa were lighting cigarettes at the bottom of the steps when she felt him come out of the church. It was like it was happening inside her. She waited, talking to Vanessa while he greeted people and stopped on the steps above them. In the meeting, she'd sat far to the right of him so she could watch him. Often he sat with his elbow on the back of the pew and his hand on his forehead, resting. . . .

"Hey, Reveren' Williams, how you doing?" Vanessa turned to him as he got to the bottom of the steps.

"All right. I didn' need to be out in the night air for *that* meeting though. I have to attend too many meetings." Vanessa nodded sympathetically.

"Listen," she said suddenly, "we got the second choir from Mount Pleasant to come out to the church Tuesday."

"Good. You oughta bring Mrs. Wilder out to our church. She's probably never been in the country."

Vanessa nodded, and Connie watched him, the light from the street lamp hitting his face, and the smoky, cavalier, gambler personality suddenly emerging from the preacher's.

"They've opened the new superburger place." Ward came out of the shadows and stood next to Vanessa.

"Let's integrate it," Connie said.

"Yes, let's do something for the community," Reverend Williams.

"Integration project, everyone." Ward went from group to group coercing, and people climbed into their cars and drove off.

"Do you have a car, Mrs. Wilder?" Reverend Williams' voice warming her.

"Yes I do," regretting it.

"I don't suppose you'd care to ride with me anyway. . . ."

"Not . . . ," she looked at him, "this time."

"Your pleasure."

When they got inside the superburger house, everyone—customers, waitresses and the hostess—looked up. There were fifteen of them, eleven black and four white. Connie was standing just in front of the three musketeers: Reverend Williams, Reverend Gabriel Horn and Reverend T. C. Moran. T. C. had told her that Reverend Williams called them that. Turning back to look at them now, she saw them that way, and she felt each of them fold an atmosphere around himself, deposit a shell that shock and hatred couldn't penetrate, and she felt her own form, felt herself form it, her skin toughened by calcium, as if the process had been going on all her life. The place was cold, the air conditioning turned up for the opening. The lights were bright, and the tables were filled with paper-thin white people, remote . . . then the hostess said something to her because she was in front, and she was following the hostess while the men came afterward, and it was their atmosphere enfolding her, and she walked on water to their table and sat down. A waitress appeared then with menus. Piped in Muzak played beyond the world they inhabited, and Reverend Williams was sitting directly across from her.

"Anyone care for a drink?" he asked, glancing at her.

"No." She shook her head. "Just a superburger and black coffee."

"Make the lady's coffee very black," he said to the waitress, and Connie stared at the gold wedding band gleaming against his dark hand.

They sat drinking their black coffee and eating the thick hamburgers between toasted slices of dark bread, and someone brought up the problem of getting people to register, and he asked her suddenly:

"What do you think our best approach would be, Mrs. Wilder?"

"Well, I guess start with the usual door-to-door voter registration drive . . . ," but the impact of his voice made her interrupt herself and look up from her food as Vanessa, at the end of the table, started talking, and his eyes were blazing, and his face had turned absolutely sensual, and she had never felt so stripped and desired, the force . . . and Vanessa's words went on at a distance while his face gained fire and the intensity of his lust grew, and she felt her eyes get hot, and she didn't break the glance, because she wanted him like that too, and they sat there while three eternities passed by them, and she

86

thought that his eyes were hers, and there must be nothing in the world beyond this.

And then he turned to Vanessa with his exquisite aristocratic manner, and said, "Yes, Mrs. Franklin, I think your idea shows admirable insight."

And as her power of sight came back to her, she realized that T. C. was smiling, had been watching, and in his eyes was the knowledge of a world where many things had happened.

CHAPTER 13

There was a life that she lived between the times that she saw him, but it was of almost no consequence unless she could somehow connect it with him. Before she'd met him, the focus of her life had been civil rights and community work. Now their paths had crossed, the work included him, and that whole part of her life acquired a new complexity. It was as if she had slipped into another life.

Her other life included walking to her school in the morning after she dropped the children at theirs; she watched what was happening on campus as if it existed at some immeasurable distance from her. The weather was as close to really cold as it ever got in Florida, and she wore her coat to school with the collar turned up, knowing that in another week it might suddenly turn warm again.

Some nights she went to the library while Alan sat with the kids. Work was piling up. There were term papers she was neglecting because of the needs of the people. At the end of the term, there would be finals. From the library window, high up, blocks of light shone onto the sidewalks below, and the shadows of branches fell across the light. She walked along the sidewalks toward the library, a huge cool vault, like a safe. . . .

Litany. Refuge. As the new experience took her over, she found herself sitting in the library wishing that she were in a church at a meeting. Once every few days, there would be a meeting somewhere, and she would get into the car and drive out into the darkness at night, with a miraculous sense of freedom washing over her.

This particular night, because the carburetor in her car was broken, Alan dropped her off at the church, and he and the kids went to the movies. There were very few people inside the church when she went up the steps, and so she sat on the wall outside and lighted a cigarette, looking across the street at the shacks, darkened except for the gray glow of TV screens shining through windows.

His car shot along the street, long and sleek and black, with a white top. He parked it, got out and came toward her, slowly.

"Evenin', Mrs. Wilder."

"Good evening, Reverend."

"How you doing?"

"Fine."

"Where's your car? I didn't see it."

"The carburetor's broken. I need a way to get home. Would you mind taking me?" Too precipitate, rushed, not the way he would have done it.

"No, not at all," with a consummate courtesy that implied that nothing lurked behind it. She got up then, and they went up the stairs and into the meeting. He went and sat by T. C., and she sat with some women she knew slightly. She sat taking notes on the locations of the various polling places, on the hours possible for registration, and thinking about him and wondering what lay ahead for her.

It was possible, she thought, that she'd made the whole thing up, that he wasn't really interested, that, like so much else around, it was fiction. The heat told tales. People sat on the porches of their houses and spun fantastic lives around the passers-by. Fifteen kinds of infamy in the palm of your hand. In the dark, sheltered depths of back-country roads lurked fortunetellers and root women, spells that could be cast in a moment and ruin a life. She didn't know how much of any of it she believed. Memories of her friend Carmen Rivera in New York, of gypsy fortunetellers, she didn't know how much of it she believed, but she was discovering within herself a capacity for belief that she hadn't known she had, and the idea of spells and root women drew her like a series of magnets held in darkness away from the light, bright squares of classrooms at the university, away from the clipped, brittle conversation of the faculty wives over coffee or cocktails, away from everything she'd thought was real between the covers of books, at gatherings of intellectual people where ideas were exchanged. She felt as if someone were digging at her soul in an attempt to find out what was inside.

After the meeting, she went over and got into his car and sat there waiting for him. He got in, and they drove off, from the dirt roads to the paved roads, and along one of the main streets.

"I'm exhausted," she said. "I've been doing too much."

"Well, don't then. Look at what happened to me. I ended up sick in the hospital from working too much."

"It wouldn't be that with me. With me, it would be a nervous breakdown."

"You're too valuable for that. We can't afford to lose you. You have to be strong in this world, no nervous breakdowns."

They weren't driving toward her house, and she wasn't sure he knew where her house was, but she didn't say anything. They turned off the main street onto a quiet tree-lined street where there were only a few lights, and he took her hand, casually, almost as if he were going to look at her rings, but then he held it.

"I've thought about you for so long," and he looked at her.

"We haven't known each other for that long," feeling shy, feeling the need to make at least token resistance, real resistance being beyond her.

"Maybe I was thinking about you even before I saw you and didn't realize it."

"I don't know, I just don't know."

"You don't know what?" He was amused. The atmosphere in the car was different, the air was charged, the car was a world.

"Maybe I don't know what I'm doing here," as if she looked to him to explain it to her.

"Do you feel sorry you're here?" his hand enclosing hers, his thumb going across the back of her hand . . .

"More like lucky," softly, and disturbed and confused. She leaned her head against the back of the seat to relieve some of the pressure inside, and she closed her eyes. "How old are you?" she asked, as if she were coming slowly out of an imagined world and into the real one.

"Why do you want to know that?"

"I just think it's important."

"Fifty-eight. Is that too old?" He turned to her again, the eternally ironic expression in his eyes.

"No, it's not that. It's just that I wanted you to be honest."

"And I was. I would be doing our relationship a disservice if I weren't."

Relationship . . . he was driving slowly now, and they were just looking at each other; then he reached over and put his hand on her breast, gently, watching her as if he expected her to withdraw.

"We're crazy," she said softly.

"*I'm* crazy?"

"*We're* crazy."

"Good. I'm going to take you home now, but I want to see you soon. Will you call me at T. C.'s tomorrow?"

"I don't want to call you at T. C.'s."

"Why not?"

"It would look funny."

"It needn't."

"I'll see."

"Sleep well."

"You too."

She got out of the car and walked into the house. The living room was half dark, and Alan was sitting on the couch listening to Beethoven's Seventh. She sat down on the couch next to him, put her head back and let the music float her.

"How was the meeting?" he asked her finally.

"Routine. Organizational. How was the movie?"

"Okay for the kids, strictly for the kids."

"That's too bad."

He nodded, got up. "I'm going to bed."

"I'll be in in a minute."

She sat there turning her hand over, looking at it . . . what was there in the way he held her hand, in the way he did everything, a sense of possession. He circled in on his desires like a hawk, his prey the world. He looked at her, and her world changed. She sighed, got up and took the record off. What would anyone she knew in Berkeley or New York say if they heard she was falling for a preacher. The world rested on irony, rested and balanced there. . . .

CHAPTER 14

Afternoons at T. C.'s. Drinking Cokes and discussing philosophy, religion, culture, politics and personalities. Sitting on a broken car seat and holding hands when no one was looking. Waiting each time to see if he would get there. And talking endlessly about the problem of finding a bed.

T. C. gave her a piece of newspaper, and she put it down on the entrance to the shed and sat on it. Her books were scattered on the car seat where she'd dropped them when she came in; her children were at school, and she felt a kind of liquid freedom. An old man sat on the car seat smoking and saying nothing. T. C. was leaning against one of the wooden supports of the lean-to drinking a Coke.

"My niece still in your dance class?"

"She didn't come this week," scratching in the dust with a stick, wondering if he'd have time to come. Now he was out building, after that he had a funeral to attend, then a meeting.

"She couldn't this week. They hauled her up."

"Where?"

"She'll go to the reform school soon's they have a place for her. Right now they got her in the jail."

"What for?"

"Skippin' school."

"Jesus." Connie felt her anger mount. "They got another of my dancers, Coretha Jones, for violation of curfew, six months!" She thought now of Castelle McClure, fourteen, beautiful and vulnerable. The shafting of innocents. Now her sense of outrage was huge and continual because the shafting here went on with a hard regularity and only the black people got shafted.

The phone rang. T. C. went into the shed to answer it: "T. C. Moran's Repair Shop . . . yeah? . . . Sure . . . I know, child. . . . Y'know I'll do what I can . . . ," T. C. answering one of the many cries for help that came to him more regularly than paying customers.

She felt she ought to say something to the old man. "Nice day," she said.

"Yep, sure is." There were people in the black community, *many* of them, who would never see her as a human being but simply forever stigmatized as a white woman.

She looked away from the old man just in time to see the car pull into the yard in one smooth motion. "Hi."

"Hi." He got out of the car and walked slowly toward her. He was wearing his work clothes, a green shirt, work pants, heavy boots, and he walked like a bull elephant. He belonged up and out, on a throne or in the jungle. Things got too small for him, had always been, and she could see in his eyes sometimes that he was ready to knock it all down. His father had been born a slave, and if there was such a thing as noble stock, then by rights his father should have been a king.

"How you doin', Mrs. Wilder?"

"Fine."

"Mr. Bell?"

"Okay, Rev, how you doin'?"

"Been buildin'. I'm tired." He sat down on a rusty chair next to her. "Got a funeral at two-thirty and a meeting of the Human Rights Commission at five."

"How's that going?"

"A farce!" His face took on the cast of his anger. "They ain't out to accomplish anything, and they ain't about to accomplish anything. I fight 'em everytime I'm down there. Everytime a case comes up involving discrimination, ol' man Patterson says, perhaps the person isn't qualified for the job. There ain't a single black person working at City Hall now except for a janitor, and they say that's not discrimination. Girl I know's been to business college, four years, she had a good position as a secretary in New York. Came home, went to City Hall, an' they didn' hire her. Shoot, if that ain't discrimination, nothing is."

"Want a Coke?" She handed him one.

He pulled a hammer out of his belt and opened the bottle. "Thanks. I tell you, I'm ready to quit that thing."

"Why'd the girl want to leave New York?" Connie asked him.

He laughed. "You're so crazy." He turned to Mr. Bell. "This girl thinks everybody's just dying to get to New York or Chicago or one of them other big dirty cities."

Mr. Bell shook his head as if it confirmed his worst sus-

94

picions. "You see, Mrs. Wilder"—Reverend Williams looked at
her, amusement in his eyes—"we who've lived here don't go
for those cities. Too much noise, not enough time to think
things out. Life is wild enough here without going to the cities."

She was beginning to find that out.

T. C. came out of the shed. "Hey, Rev, how you doin'?"

"Fine. You?"

"Not good. That was Fontana. They got Castelle down in
the jailhouse; she been there three days."

Reverend Williams shook his head slowly.

"Soons I get my clothes on, I gotta go calm Fontana down."
He went back into the inside room of the shed and closed the
door.

"That's two kids I know in the last couple of months,"
Connie said, "and they're both just babies. . . ." The sickness
within her was deep and permanent.

Reverend Williams nodded, and his nod was more than
whatever words she might have chosen; always behind his voice,
his eyes, his gestures was the weight of what he'd seen and
the wisdom with which he'd assessed it.

"What can we do?" she asked him.

"Probably nothing." He lighted a cigarette and gazed out at
the wrecked cars in the yard. "But T. C.'ll find out, and then,
well, I'll mention it at this thing this afternoon, not that that'll
do any good, and then maybe we can think about some sort
of action." He sighed.

"Well"—Mr. Bell got up with admirable slowness—"I'm
fixin' to go. World ain't gettin' no better here."

"That's for sure," Connie said.

"We'll see ya, Mr. Bell."

She was learning the tones of his voice. There was a layer
over it now, and beneath that layer was his desire for Mr. Bell
to go so they could, in some relative sense, be alone.

"You're so pretty." He turned to her as soon as Mr. Bell got
out of the yard.

She smiled. "What's new with our problem?"

"Nothing, but I'm working on something." He got up and
went up the steps of the shed. She sat there, still feeling his

eyes burn through her. "Hey, come in here a minute." He gestured. She went up the steps and inside. He closed the door behind her and put her up against it. Then he kissed her, slowly, slowly, slowly, and his hands went over her body. "Oh, honey, we gotta find someplace to go."

"I know." She felt her desire down through her back and in her hips.

"Connie." He put his hands to her face and looked at her, saw into her depths. "Connie, you know I love you." Flame and fuse and melting fire, everything within her turned to flame, she loved him, but she was afraid to let it be said, to hear it in the open air. She felt her being throb in response to his.

"You don't have to say that," with her remaining defenses. "You've got me already."

"I know I've got you." He said it softly. "I've known it since that night in the restaurant. I never tell a woman I love her when I don't. It causes too much pain, but I *love* you, honey," his voice warming her, causing so much wonder in her.

"I love you too," and before his mouth tasted hers again, "too much."

CHAPTER 15

Coretha Jones was considered a criminal because she'd been caught walking home with her boyfriend at eleven o'clock in the evening. Coretha did not have Castelle's problem with school; she went pretty regularly partly because she was already a year behind due to the fact that she had spent her fifth-grade year by her mother's bedside, when her mother had had tuberculosis. Her mother had died.

Castelle McClure was considered a criminal because she'd skipped school a lot. Castelle had been kept in jail for two weeks because there wasn't any place for juveniles to go when the reform school was full. Coretha had been lucky; she'd been sent to the reform school right away. Connie took some of their relatives up to see them almost every Sunday. Today she was with Fontana and two of her sons. The boys had a transistor in the back, and the music blared through the car, out the windows and into the November air—"Papa's Got a Brand-New Bag"—with its insistent beat, music that had seemed so strange to her when she'd first heard it that she hadn't even liked it, and now she felt it as a part of her blood....

"One a my boys in the jailhouse too." Fontana broke the silence.

Connie turned to her; the depth of other people's pain, but Fontana was just sitting there. Connie watched her . . . ; if you were going to help people, you couldn't drown in their pain, couldn't romanticize it. "Why is he in jail?"

Fontana shrugged. "He didn' have some kinda identification papers he needed, thass what they say."

"Identification papers?"

"The poh-lice don' like us, never did, not none of us, McClures, Morans an' Johnsons."

"We'll have to see what we can do about the paper business," Connie said. Driving through a wide green Florida prairie to the reform school. Overhead the sky stretched; there was more of a space of sky in Florida than anywhere else she'd been, a huge, curving vaulted piece of sky with heavy masses of bright, white clouds, the rich spill of the weather incongruous in a land so loaded with pain, but the weather, like the people, could be violent and vivid, curtains of rain and living towers of heat . . . there were depths here, and the water turned dark and tropical with bright gold- and orange-colored fish swimming among weeds at the bottom. . . . Her feelings towered like the heat and fell like the rain. She lived in a torrent of feeling.

"Probly can't do nothin'," Fontana said, and looked out the window again, " 'cept pray."

I wish there was a God, Connie thought. T. C. and Jason were trying to convert her. Jason said he never thought of her as an atheist.

"If his daddy was livin', wouldn' have happened," Fontana went on.

"How long has he been dead?"

From the back of the car, Sam Cooke singing "A Change Is Gonna Come"; Lucinda Williams was going to dance to it in the next recital.

" 'Bout five year. Can't get over how it happen though."

"How'd it happen?"

"Well, ya know the girl had a baby for my oldes' boy?"

Connie nodded.

"That girl mother a root woman, bad as the devil hisself, with eyes like glass. There was a card game over to her house, an' she got my man drunk on that shine, an' he was the las' one there, she saw to that, an' she said she saw the sign on him so she slit his wrists and put him in a locked room and let him bleed to death for three days."

"My God." She'd heard the story before, in various garbled versions, but she hadn't been sure it was true.

"Castelle was the one found him. Broke a window in the place 'cause she saw a body, jes a body in an empty room. He always did take up for Castelle though. She was his favorite." They drove on, and Fontana was silent, and there was only the sound of the motor and the beat of the music from the transistor, and Connie thought about her introduction to the occult, about Carmen Rivera and Madame Fanlia. . . .

. . . She had met Carmen working for the agency in New York that sent the kids to camp. Carmen worked at the Center, where Juan lived, and the rest of them, Bernard, Luvenia and she herself, worked back and forth between the Center and their downtown office. Carmen did not hang out with them a lot; Juan said Carmen was a snob and didn't want to be with other Puerto Ricans, words he rolled off his tongue in the Spanish of his childhood, but she and Carmen had somehow become close. Connie knew that Juan was right; Carmen dated all kinds of weird people, and most of them were wealthy. She and Juan both wanted out, but Juan knew he had to do it by his own brainpower; Carmen was willing to go out on the coattails of a rich man. The first thing you had to deal with about Carmen was her beauty; at eighteen Carmen was so beautiful that, even on New York's busy streets, men stopped and turned around and followed her for blocks just to watch her walk. She walked like the ocean moving, sensual and full and regular; every step suggested sexuality, but she wasn't coming on to any particular man, she simply existed, like the original woman. Her hair was black and fell in heavy waves three inches below her shoulders, her eyes were a dark, dark brown and her complexion was café au lait. She was color and motion, Connie thought, at their most essential, and there was no stopping her.

But her beauty did have its drawbacks; if Juan de la Torres used being a Puerto Rican in New York City as a justification for his total and permanent militance, Carmen used it as a reminder that, although she was a beautiful woman, there were a limited number of things she could do with that beauty. And so her retreat into the occult was made in a desperate attempt to wrench meaning from a world that had created her in the image of a goddess and tinged that image of beauty with sin in the eyes of a million uptight Americans before Carmen even stepped out the door. . . . And the occult was only one path that Carmen took into the mystery. The other was the path into the world of the Catholic church, in which she'd been raised, and Father Ramirez, with whom Connie had worked, stood there, wise and generous, trying to deal with

Carmen's impatience with the world, but he was not enough. He could not deal, to Carmen's satisfaction, with the world of the poem that her little brother José had written:

On the street where you live
Also live the Ruiz', Ortiz', Ramos', Rodriguez', Ramirez'
    and Hernandez'
On the street where you live
Also live eighteen dope addicts, hooked to their eyeballs,
        jazzing up bags of uneaten, barely cooked bones,
                junkies by night.
On the street where you live
Also live rats, large as cats, with furry, soot-dark bodies,
        disgusting and vicious, like you.

Father Ramirez would work himself to the bone to change conditions, and tell her that she must be patient and tell her to pray. Out of frustration, Carmen at fifteen, had started going to Madame Fanlia's to learn gypsy tricks and hear tales of the occult. On the dirty window of the shop was a cardboard sign that proclaimed in red letters: "Madame Fanlia Knows the Future."

"Well, she certainly knows something," Carmen said, "and whatever it is, I plan to learn it." Gradually she initiated Connie into the mysteries. Madame Fanlia was not a pure priestess; she called innocence the ability to be taken, and found its seed in ignorance, ignorance of things people didn't mind too much not knowing about, because they weren't sure they existed, and she was willing to take the tourists, for that was how she made her money. But with Carmen, she was serious, and she told Carmen that she had the power to make her an adept and that Carmen had the talent; she wanted Carmen to sell her her soul so that she could train it.

"I don't know," Connie said. "It sounds risky to me."

"But she said it wouldn't hurt, and it's only temporary. Once she's trained it, it will slip back into my body so quietly that I won't even notice it. Anyway . . . ," Carmen interrupted herself to sip her Coke. They were having lunch at a counter place halfway between the agency office and Madame Fanlia's shop. "Anyway, she said if I wanted to, I could bring a friend while she does it, if I was scared, and I've decided to bring you." It was a great honor, Connie knew, but she felt an involuntary chill flow through her body.

"Wow," she said, "I'd like to, but what if I'm scared?"

"She's not going to do it to you. There's no reason for you to be scared."

"Okay." It was an act of friendship, and Connie never resisted those. She was also curious.

"Okay, Saturday, at ten o'clock. You come to my house and get me." Connie nodded, and they got up to go back to work.

On Saturday, Carmen was ready early and waiting at the bottom of the steps of the brownstone when Connie came by. Connie hadn't told her parents where she was going; she could feel their worlds parting. The comfortable apartment house on Central Park West, the furniture, the carpets and her mother and father's attitudes—they all seemed irrelevant. So she had taken an apple from the icebox and left the house before they were up; that had left her with two hours to kill, and she had wandered over to Times Square and looked in store windows and read books in the open bookstores, heat and the glorious morning air of New York before people had gotten to it . . .

"Are you ready?" Connie asked her.

"Yes, but feel my hands." She put her hands in Connie's; they were ice cold.

"You sure you want to do this?"

Carmen nodded, and they started walking down Ninth Avenue toward Forty-first Street, where Madame Fanlia's shop was. All the grocery stores were open now, the Saturday shoppers already in them, poring over the foods, seeing what they could get that would be cheap enough to feed the family.

The room at Madame Fanlia's was small and square; there was a chair in the corner and two chairs placed next to a small round table covered with a piece of red oilcloth, on which stood a small clear glass globe with a candle burning in it. At the back of the shop, there were faded red curtains concealing the entrance to another room. It was through these curtains that Madame Fanlia came now.

"Carmen," she said, her voice warm, almost reassuring. "And this is your friend?"

Carmen introduced them.

"You will sit over there," she told Connie.

Connie nodded, relieved to be able to retreat to the corner.

Madame Fanlia was thin and old, her hands were wrinkled and bony, but there was something skillful about them. Her eyes, dark and shrewd and somehow not wholly seeing you, were the striking feature in her thin, wrinkled face. Her long skirt and denim shirt looked like they had come from the Goodwill store, and around her head she wore a rag turban stuck full of bobby pins, inauspicious, unpropitious, Connie thought, but, then, what did she know about the occult?

Carmen and Madame Fanlia were seated opposite each other at the table, and Connie could almost begin to feel some of the woman's force; it was as if, once she was at that table, her powers heightened her energy, allowing her to transcend herself so that she became beautiful and fired with the single passion of her knowledge of what lay at the center of all the mysteries. . . .

"All right," Madame Fanlia said, "how much do you want me to pay you?"

"Five dollars?" Carmen shrugged her shoulders.

"All right, but your soul is worth millions, no price can be put on it, it is beyond the values which mortals possess. I give you this money so that you may know I am serious." She searched among the folds of her skirt for the pocket where she kept her money. "Here." She gave the bill to Carmen. "Now write on a slip of paper the date and what you have done. Then sign it and give it to me."

Carmen bent over the table and wrote out the slip of paper and gave it to Madame Fanlia. Madame Fanlia took it, and Connie could hear the sound of each of her gold bracelets hitting the others as she moved her hands. Madame Fanlia took the paper and stuck the corner of it into the candle flame . . . , and the paper writhed into its dark shape, and then Madame Fanlia broke it between her fingers into flakes of black, which dropped from her smudged fingertips into the globe holding the candle and floated inside on the surface of the hot, melted wax, and all the time Madame Fanlia's mobile mouth worked, murmuring incantations.

Then finally she said: "Your soul is in the air. It is floating upward and filling the room."

And Carmen stood up as if she was pulled up, and Connie watched the expression of sudden pain on her face and swore forever afterward that she felt the whole wooden structure of the room shake as she watched Carmen stand there trembling with her head thrown back, and there was something in the room that she could feel almost as if it was substance, currents of powerful force breaking on the walls, and Carmen went up on her toes, and her arms went up almost convulsively, and her mouth went open, and she stood there, poised, for what seemed to Connie an eternity, and Connie could feel darkness in the room; the room seemed to get darker, and it was as if darkness was pouring in and out of Carmen, as if she were a medium through which rivers passed, and Carmen came down off her toes and fell to her knees, and Connie could see the sweat pouring off her and the tears running down her face. . . . "Your soul is full of pain and beauty, beauty and pain, your life is at the outer reaches, and you will have to choose in your life between money and wisdom, you will be offered a lot of money one way or another, but I will try and train your soul to make choices . . . you must always be careful about the way money lures you, and you must be careful to learn wisdom with men, for men will not be able to be wise around you, you will need every power I can give you. . . ." There was a pause, and Connie could almost feel some of the pressure leave the room. "Carmen, that's enough," and Carmen got up off her knees, wiped her face with a tissue that Madame Fanlia produced from one of her pockets and looked exhausted.

They walked slowly back to Carmen's house.

"Do you feel any different?" Connie asked her after they had walked a block in silence.

"Yes," Carmen said. "Clean and quiet and refreshed and whole."

"But do you feel like you're missing anything? After all, that was your soul that got out in there."

"She told me it would be like that; I'm quieter temporarily without it. My soul needs quieting. I'm too turbulent and violent."

Connie nodded.

"Connie," Carmen said after a minute, "did you feel anything of what was happening?"

"Yes," Connie said, and described all the pressures and the shaking of the room.

"Connie," Carmen said, "I *felt* my soul leave my body; it was like a physical pain almost when it wrenched free. It just eased out, and that's when I went up on my toes, like strings were pulling me up." She looked shocked.

"Yeah," Connie said, "it was really something."

They had reached Carmen's house, and they said good-bye feeling that something in the ceremony had bound them together forever. And Carmen was quieter after that, quieter and almost less vibrant, and didn't go out with as many rich boys.

One day, she and Connie went into the bathroom at Grand Central, and Carmen said: "Connie, I got it back. I'm all together again, and I have all kinds of new insights," and Connie nodded, and that was all they ever said about it. . . .

. . . They drove past churches, unpainted wooden structures set back from the road; large shiny cars were parked in front of them: gleaming white Cadillacs, long sleek Pontiacs, the only sign in a materially depleted world that here was a black man who'd made it. Beside the long cars stood the old cars, long cars and wrecks; Reverend Williams said that his car was part of his personality.

They passed another church, Fontana singing softly beside her now, some Sunday song, brother a preacher, deep roads cut into the soul. The cars stood outside the church, quiet and well behaved, and inside the spirit was climbing the walls, maybe right now someone in that church had it, maybe some-

104

one was walking the pews. There was a large part of her dying to be converted in some total way, the same part of her that had longed to ask Madame Fanlia if she would buy her soul too, so that she might become an adept . . . the door into the mystery . . .

CHAPTER 16

On Saturday nights, they generally went out, she and Alan, to other faculty members' houses or with other faculty members to restaurants. There were not many good restaurants in Orangedale, and they talked about that. There was not much good liquor in Orangedale, and they talked about that. Nor were there plays, operas, concerts or museums of great note. This too was an endless topic of conversation among sophisticated people who had lived in cities. Politics of the *U.S. News & World Report* to *Newsweek* to *New Republic* variety loomed large. Some of the faculty members and their wives were intellectuals, and those who weren't pretended to be.

This Saturday night, Connie was tired, and she sat in a corner drinking her drink and watching. She was wearing a black dress, and all week she'd spent her free time and much of her time that wasn't free working on Castelle McClure's and Coretha Jones' cases, and she felt as if she were in mourning, black shoes, black dress. Once, she'd belonged with these people, or they'd had something to do with her, but now they had nothing to do with her because everything that consumed her mind was alien to them. . . .

"In Orangedale, you know, you really can't get very many clothes. The children can, of course. . . ."

"I go to Tampa, myself. I go once every three months. You ought to come with me."

"I go to Jacksonville."

"Oh?"

"I go to Tallahassee."

Or, from the men: "Well, that Harry Evans they're considering is no good at all. I know already that I'm going to vote against him."

"Did you hear the story he told about 'nigras'. He doesn't realize the kind of group he's in here. He must've thought it was the deep South." Laughter, and the man who'd spoken let his eyes slide across her face, waiting for her reaction, wanting her silent approval. They considered her their link with the black community, and so they asked her questions the answers to which they weren't really interested in, and, at the same time, they became more guarded with her daily. They watched her as if they hoped to be able to read her mind by watching and, through her mind, to be able to get at the elusive truths of the time, what black people *wanted*, as if her mind were a filter, as if the truths were elusive.

"These canapés are just delicious. What's in them?"

"Just that onion-soup mix and sour cream."

If they could have read her mind tonight, they would have read only his image and the fact that loomed in her near future: I am about to become his mistress. There would have been nothing in any of their white middle-class lives that would have prepared them for that fact or for the states that her soul encountered in other people every day, the states that her soul was struggling to attain. So many human virtues that had long gone out of style: generosity, sharing, the sort of love that Vanessa had the power of, so that she could enter a room and the love would pour forth from her like light and all the people would be warmed and eased. But if she would love like Vanessa, she must give up contempt. In order to love people freely, one had to give up, at one level, the passionate taking of sides, and therein lay the paradox and the explanation of why revolutionaries gave up their religion and why mystics remained detached from what was conventionally called revolution.

But he! Therein lay a deeper paradox still, one she couldn't resolve, his personal paradox. He did both. He was both the spiritual and the political leader, an angered side taker and a pure giver from the heart. No, he was beyond—anything.

She too, like the other people in this room, was sitting there eating sour cream and onion-soup-mix dip on potato chips, and when the dinner was announced, she too arose and lined up at a card table made to double as a buffet table and helped herself to a pile of some kind of goulash and a serving of tossed salad and hot rolls and a small glass of red wine. The evening was an awkward sitting of people on chairs, awkwardly eating while being aware of eating and trying to drink enough so that at least they could take the edge off the tension they felt just by virtue of the fact that they sat together eating. Her mind slid off to the years of this kind of gathering that lay behind her and the infinite years that lay ahead. Her being was torn by her desire to be where T. C. was now, to be with Vanessa but most of all to be with the Reverend Jason H. Williams, who seemed to have an inexhaustible supply of feeling. The more time she spent with black people, the less real most white people became to her. Ultimately you didn't choose; you were selected, slotted, allocated to a certain role in life. Yet there were a few moments in your life when you were given the chance to choose, and for her, this was becoming one of them. Paradoxically, real choice was not choice, for there was no moment when your mind made a decision, but something happened to you internally at so deep a level that your being moved after that happening, and your mind and body followed like shadows the motion of your soul—Carmen Rivera on tiptoe with her arms raised as her soul eased out of her body.

"How are things on the civil rights scene, Connie?" jerked back to reality by the sound of a voice.

"Fine," and what kind of answer was that? But what kind of question had it been? His name was Earl Osborne, and he was in the law school, and he seemed to her to be waging some kind of campaign to keep that fact at the front of your mind.

"I see you on the picket lines all the time. I've seen your picture in the papers."

She nodded. What was she expected to say now? Yes, I was there?

He laughed into his drink, his shoulders hunching awkwardly as he laughed. "You know what they're saying about you," smiling slowly, the secret lurking behind his smile.

"No. In fact, I don't even know who *they* are."

"*They.*" He gestured with his hands, the eloquence of his gestures derived from the courtroom. "The great public, they before whom we perform all our lives. They are saying that there's this girl named Connie Wilder, who's a wild-haired radical, and that she's married to Alan Wilder, who's a brilliant young lawyer and a nice guy to boot, and that the aforementioned Connie is going to ruin the lawyer Alan's career."

"Well, I'm glad they've found something to keep their minds occupied with and you've found something to keep your mouth moving," and she got up and walked slowly over to a group where some women were discussing toilet training, and she listened, knowing she shouldn't have let out that flood of hostility.

"Let's go." Alan came up behind her. She got her coat, and they mumbled elaborate insincere thanks to the couple who'd given the dinner. Outside, the darkness was cool, and she let the cool air ride down her arms before she put her coat on.

"Why so silent?" They had driven halfway home already, and she'd spent the time looking out the window, trying to take in the town outside, trying to realize that the house they'd just visited was in the same town where *he* lived.

"No reason, just tired I guess." If she told him about Earl Osborne, he'd be angry. And with reason. He had to work with Earl, but people pushed her. Now, on their way home, they were on a main street, and a block beyond it was a dirt road and the church where she'd been a few weeks before, the night he'd first driven her home, two worlds, the black and the white crushed together in a tiny town and almost totally unmixed.

CHAPTER 17

The lure of dark roads. She followed him down them time after time, to a meeting place where they talked for five minutes and he kissed her good night. Impelled to risk a great deal for very little, they kept driving. There was always the fear of cops, and one night she drove down a dirt road and saw a car parked with its lights dimmed, and she thought it was him. When she got close, driving slowly, with the danger of the half unknown always ahead, the lights of the car went up, and it was a cop. She drove more quickly then, and he seemed to be following her until she got to the main road, but then he disappeared. Black cop, lucky; there were only three in town, but you never knew who you could trust. She was a white woman driving alone through a black neighborhood late at night. She drove back around and down another road, and his car came along the other way. Slowly they drew up next to each other. Their cars made love because they couldn't.

"Hey," he said.

"Hi, I saw a cop."

"Go on home. I'll call you in the morning."

"I can't take much more of this."

"Neither can I. I'll think of something."

"Okay."

She drove home through the darkness where the Spanish moss cast shadows into empty space and built phantoms in the air. The world was a dark, fear-laden place, each street lamp giving you only half a chance to detect what lay ahead. She was doing all this because she loved him, while the solid plaster mind of her past said no. Yet that mind was loosening, people were beginning to replace ideas, passion was beginning to replace reason, life was beginning to replace books. She went home to read Henry James.

The next night, she followed him down the highway leading out of town, and the roads, in their hung darkness, opened up. She followed him to the edge of town and out into the country, down dirt road after dirt road until they hit a narrow, bumpy road which he drove his smooth car down slowly. Here there were only their car lights, hers following his, and the light cast up into the hanging moss, and the sense of a

111

deep tunnel that they entered and went farther and farther into, until finally he stopped in a clearing where the trees hung silently around them. The only sound once their motors were turned off was the distant bark of a dog. She got out of her car and went over to his. He opened the door for her, and she got in.

"Hello," she said.

"Hello, baby," and she moved into his arms. "Oh baby I want you."

"I want you," her hands on his face, their mouths together, their eyes exploring each other's depths in some absolute and frightening way. She took his hand and kissed it. "I do that because I honor you," she said.

"Crazy girl." He took a handful of her hair and tipped her head back so he could kiss her neck. "One of the reasons I love you is that you're such a crazy girl."

"Listen." She put her hands to his face again. "Louis Lomax said that this year a lot of white women would be sleeping with black men in order to prove something to themselves. I thought when I read that that I might be one of those women."

"No, darling, you'd only sleep with a man you loved." Final. He was one of the few people she'd met who was way ahead of her about people, and he was the only person she'd met who was way ahead of her about herself.

"I know that now." She opened her dress to him, and he pushed her bra up over her breasts and put his hands on her and kissed her nipples. She watched him and held his head against her. "I want to give myself to you—now."

He looked at her. "Darlin', I can't take you here. We've gotta wait. I got a sermon to write tonight." It was like a bell that had been under water suddenly surfacing and ringing. He had a sermon to write. His hand was on her thigh, and she could feel her face changing for him. There was sweat on his forehead. "Do you love me?" he asked her.

"Yes, oh yes," with tremors going all through her.

"Then send me home to my books."

"Okay." She smiled. "Anything for the church."

He laughed.

"I don't see how it all works together though."

"Someday I'll tell you. Listen, darlin', I think I can work something out for Wednesday. That okay with you?"

She nodded.

"I've never wanted a woman the way I want you. I'm not sure what that means."

"It means I'm white."

He shook his head. "You don't give me as much credit as I give you. I've had white women, honey, it's not that."

"I'm glad." Her voice softened.

"Y'know, I don't feel that race thing exists when I'm with you. There's just you and me."

"I feel that too."

His eyes took her in, assessed what she had been and what she might become. "Yes, I know that. I think we feel pretty much the same thing, even when we don't use the same words for it, and I'm not used to that. I usually feel, alone."

"I'll go now." She kissed him and got out of his car.

"Good night, baby. Follow me home so you won't get lost."

"Okay," the car door slamming and her sudden aloneness in the dark.

The nice new homes for black people were located in a large development at one end of town, and the nice new homes for white people were located in many developments at the other end of town. Between them were sections of old, aristocratic-looking ruined frame houses, where she and Alan lived, and shacks. On Monday afternoon, after she'd gone to the store, she drove with Willie and Robin toward the nice new homes for black people because she thought from his address that that was where he lived, and she wanted to see. But she couldn't find it, and after she'd been through the development twice, she went over a few blocks and down a dirt road, and there was a house with his street address on it. It was a plain gray shack, not the smallest and not the oldest but absolutely plain and weathered. She drove slowly past, not hearing what Willie and Robin were saying. The cavalier Reverend Williams, he was that, and he was a preacher, and he gave money away more freely than anyone else she'd ever known, and he didn't have it to give, for he was also the man who lived in that shack, and he was the man whose car she'd been in Saturday night. He was, in short, a great deal more than she'd bargained for.

PART FOUR

THE PREACHER'S CORNER

He had just gotten in the door when the phone rang. It generally did ring enough so that it was impossible for him to get any work done in his office. . . . It was Connie on the phone, her low voice coming from another world, washing into his ear like sea water. She made his heart ache most of the time, reminding him of the forgotten and the impossible. . . .

He returned to his text:

Vanity of vanities, saith the Preacher, vanity of vanities,
all is vanity. . . .

I communed with mine own heart, saying, Lo, I am come to great estate, and have gotten more wisdom than all they that have been before me in Jerusalem: yea, my heart had great experience of wisdom and knowledge.

And I gave my heart to know wisdom, and to know madness and folly: I perceived that this also is vexation of spirit.
For in much wisdom is much grief: and he that increaseth knowledge increaseth sorrow. . . .

And he found himself in the passage. He wondered sometimes at how hard he'd worked to learn what he'd learned; now he could feel the suffering of more people than he'd once been able to. He sat there and thought about pain, looked out upon his world and then went out into it, stretched his hand out to his people, watched hope rise in their faces, light, whatever made life worth living, so much hope extended to each person until he was drained.

He had wondered about what had been entrusted to him. He knew that he had been called, he even knew the moment at which that calling had been made manifest. He had fought being called until the last moment, and then one day he had found himself walking around at the front of the church, saying, Thank you, Jesus, thank you, Jesus; and he had known then that the moment of choice had passed. Just as you could not question the act of being called once it had happened to you, so you could not question God's judgment in calling you. Had He wanted someone else, He would have called someone else. Everyone was available to Him. Subdued, calmed by this line of reasoning, you acquiesced. But he still wondered sometimes about the tasks that he had been called to, and he knew that he was sometimes unworthy; there had been times when his manhood had gotten the better of him and the pressure had gotten so great that he'd had a lot to drink and lain in the arms of some beautiful young woman until he could feel the pressure easing off, until he could get up and go out and struggle again with the Leviathan that he had found the world to be. Struggle and challenge and fight . . . that's how he had found the world, and the world had made him violent. For years, when he had been a young man, he had sat with his back to the wall so that he faced all the windows and doors just in case someone came busting in. When he was a young man, he never smiled or laughed much; there was an ease that came with wisdom though, and now he could smile at the world's follies, for he knew them so well, and he knew that there were times to fight. Yet you could not fight all the time; there were times when tact and diplomacy would get you farther than fighting. Wisdom and time had brought him irony.

They had also brought him Connie, who had been least expected in his life. He'd thought he was through with women, with his extracurricular activities, that he would settle down with his wife and devote himself wholly to religious study. You didn't expect to fall in love when you were fifty-eight years old. He'd thought that he'd grown into his age until she came into his life. It had happened suddenly. One day she was there, a dark-haired, slim white girl with her hair all down her back, a girl on a picket line who came out of nowhere and into a meeting all hot and burned, and looked at him with all the innocence and lack of calculation that he'd been taught by his own experience never to trust in people, particularly in white people.

There was no one just like her, and it was a strange thing when a woman became part of you, a woman you'd known three and a half months and hadn't even gone to bed with. It was a strange thing when you'd been schooled to believe that white people were a race apart. She upset him when she was disturbed about not being able to get him on the phone; then he calmed her and told her it wasn't that important, but if he didn't talk to her or see her for a couple of days, he missed her terribly, though he hardly ever told her. She had enough to go through now without having his feelings piled up on hers.

He knew that he needed to get back to his sermon, but his mind wandered. His mind was like a tramp; it wandered all over the place, lingering now and again on certain images: a thousand images of fulfillment, the things he had dreamed of as a young man but had never thought he would have were being offered to him now, when he was too old to allow himself to accept them. For, by most people's standards, he knew he was an old man, but he couldn't make himself feel it, not in any real sense. There were realistic limits to what he could do, but he could still do most of the things he had been able to do twenty years ago, and he could feel his strength when he was building or laying bricks, and knew that he was as fast and as accurate as ever. But there were things about his age he couldn't explain to Connie, just as there were things about his religion and his culture he couldn't explain to her. To him, how they could have gotten together when there were as many differences as there were between them would always be one of life's miracles, but that they were together was an incontrovertible fact as beyond question as the fact that he sat here writing a sermon, just as he had almost every Saturday afternoon for the past thirty-two years.

PART FIVE

JOURNEY TO THE CENTER OF A SOUL: DARK ROADS

Beside the road, there was a tree so shaggy with Spanish moss that it looked like a buffalo, and she and Alan were driving into a strip of deep-pink sunrise. Under that lay a strip of blue that flashed back and forth, looking for a moment like a soft, pale-blue lake they were about to drive into and then like a strip of sky, and then, when they drew close to it, they were suddenly driving through thin, white fog, and what had been a beautiful, dramatic illusion became a thick reality that they had to slow down to deal with.

Connie dug her hands into the warm pockets of her coat and leaned back and closed her eyes. The sound of the motor. If they could just keep driving forever, then she wouldn't be unfaithful to him, if she could just tell him, if she could just get on that train with him. She opened her eyes. The road ahead now flowed into a blaze of sun, rivers of light and fire. The decision had been made, and she knew that if she didn't get on that train and go with him, there would be nothing in the world that could change her mind. It was Wednesday, Alan was going away to a conference, and she had a date with Jason.

They stood on the platform, early, as usual, for the train. They were the only people there except for the station official, who bustled back and forth as if he were stationmaster at Grand Central, and Connie felt suddenly, desperately nostalgic for something in her remote past, or maybe lonely for something she'd never had.

"I hope I learn something at this conference," Alan said, and she was jerked back, her world to his world, no flow, no transition.

"I hope so too," she replied, wondering why they didn't pick up each other's vibrations.

"Because I have a lot of doubt about putting the contracts course into Leonard's hands even for a week. Things can get out of control when you don't take care of them yourself."

"Yes," she agreed, "they can." And she heard the train coming and then the heavy grinding sound as it slid its bulk to a stop in the station.

"Good-bye." He kissed her and picked up his brief case.

"And, Connie"—he looked at her—"don't work too hard, don't push yourself, let some of it go."

"Okay," she said, thinking there was still time to say something, but he was already striding away toward the train and up the steps. He was so sure, so sure of his world.

As the train pulled out, she waved to him, and driving back along the sun-filled highway, she felt she must be a different person. Wednesday. The consummation scene, and only hours to mark until nightfall.

A day of chaos, nervousness and suppressed joy. Then suddenly she found herself calmly driving down a dirt road in the tree-stilled darkness, and there was a car ahead of her, and she drove toward it as if she were going to pass it, as if she were going somewhere, and the car turned down its lights, and it was his.

"Park your car down there," he said. She did and got into his, and they drove off. He took something out of his pocket and put it on the floor in front of her feet, a brown paper bag.

"What's that?"

"A gun."

"A gun?"

"Yes." He smiled. "Most of the time you see me drivin' around, I got a gun."

"You think we'll have to use it?"

"I hope not." He turned to her. "Don't worry. I'll take good care of you."

"I know." With a certainty of safety that was new, as the danger was new. There had to be a trust greater than most people ever knew between them.

When they reached the narrowest of the dirt roads and drove slowly along under the moss, with only the headlights lighting the road ahead and the deepness of the tunnel coming at them, she slid over on the seat next to him and put her hand on the back of his neck and kissed his face and his ear. She felt she would never be able to touch him enough. He drove beyond the clearing into a yard of broken cars, wrecks etched out by the moonlight.

"What's this?" she asked him as he turned off the motor.

"See that truck over there." He pointed to a delivery truck. She nodded.

"Our bed's in there."

She smiled. "I mean, what are all these cars?"

"They're T. C.'s. This is his stockpile."

They got out of the car, and he took her in his arms, and they stood kissing among the moonlit cars, and she felt her body melt into his.

"You're my baby," he said, and the urgency came, and they went to the truck and climbed in.

The truck had a low ceiling, and there were blankets on the floor. He took off his jacket and tie and threw them over the back of the front seat.

"You like it?" he asked.

"Yes," sitting there on the floor of the truck unbuttoning her dress . . .

"You're beautiful."

"So are you."

He laughed, deep down, the way he did everything.

"Y'know," she said as she threw her dress over the seat, "in books, adultery is always very sordid."

"You take those books too seriously, honey." He gazed at her. "Isn't this sordid enough for you?"

"It isn't sordid at all. Nothing could be sordid that had anything to do with you."

He pulled her straps off her shoulders, her bra to her waist. . . . "You're beautiful," he said, and kissed her.

They moved, whirling, into a world of single sensations. He took her some way so that they fell together through some wave that carried them on and on together forever. Strange water wound deep into the patterns they made.

"Connie," he said, "darlin', love me."

And she gave him more, although she hadn't known there was anything left to give. "Oh, baby," she whispered, and there were tears in her eyes, "I do love you." Lapsed, lying together.

Later he spoke, and she could feel his voice echoing in her chest. "You'll always be part of me, even after it's over."

She rubbed her hand across his hair. "Don't talk about its being over."

"It'll happen sometime."

"But don't talk about it."

He looked at her, and she knew that he saw trouble ahead, where she saw only a blank space. "What's that?" He sat up and put his hand on his gun.

"Nothing. Leaves."

"Shhhh."

She was silent while he listened, looked out the back window, listened again and then put the gun down.

"Nothing. This time."

"You very worried?" She felt totally relaxed, and she couldn't imagine that there was a world beyond theirs.

"Honey, you can't be a black man and be reared in the South and not worry when you're with a white woman." He pulled her into his arms again.

"What do I do for you?" she asked him. "I mean besides sex, because you do so much for me."

Gently, he pushed her hair back from her forehead. "You're giving me new life, baby."

And she wanted to; they went together again, and their love was immense and grew as they moved. It was new, new like wind rising in trees at dawn, new like the green of sunlit grass, new breath, and his mouth kept going over hers, and they turned and closed further; before, she'd thought of herself as a separate person, but now she was his.

They lay there holding hands, and she could feel the power of his hand; her fingers went over his knuckles, her palm rubbed against the roughness of his palm.

"We've gotta have more light," he said. "I want to look at you. I'll try and find us a big bed next time."

"Okay," she said.

"You're a strange girl," he said reflectively. "You don't fit the notions I grew up with at all."

"You don't fit the notions I grew up with either, particularly notions about preachers."

126

"Yes, well, in your culture . . ."

"In my culture what?"

"Well, what about preachers?"

"They don't screw."

He laughed. "Ever try any?"

"No."

"Well, then you don't really *know*."

"No, but . . ."

"You assume, but assumptions are the root of all evil, and don't let anyone tell you different. C'mon, girl, get your clothes on, we gotta get out of here."

"Now?"

"It's almost twelve-thirty." He slapped her thigh.

"Okay," with the docility commanded by the situation. He knew, she didn't. "One thing . . . ," she said as she started dressing.

"What?"

"I love you."

"I love you too. Darlin', if anyone'd told me this could happen, I'd've said never."

She smiled. "One more thing . . ."

"That's you, one more thing. This is the last."

"Don't ever let me get between you and your people in any way."

"Why would you think you would?" He stopped buttoning his shirt and looked at her.

She shrugged her shoulders.

"You're a sweet girl, Connie."

"No, not sweet."

He kissed her mouth, her neck, her breasts where they rose above her slip. "Yes, sweet."

"Okay, Reverend."

"Hurry, or they might lynch us . . . ," mockery, parody.

"That's not funny." She pulled her stockings on and hooked them onto her garters.

"If *I* think it's funny, you can afford to think it's funny. I'll tell you a story someday. . . ." He knotted his tie.

She smiled, finished dressing, and they climbed out of the truck.

"It's a beautiful night," she whispered.

He took her hand. "And I'd like us to spend it together, but we can't."

Where there was an elastic stretch for her—can, can't, I have a choice—for him there were certain absolutes, cultural and religious, certain chances that couldn't be taken, certain choices he'd never been given. She felt their differences in the tone of their voices, and she obeyed him.

They'd been out on the main road for about thirty seconds when he spoke: "Pick the bag up from the floor, and take the gun out of it, then put it on the seat near my right hand. We're being followed."

The gun was cold in her hand, and after she'd put it down, she felt herself freeze. "Do you want me to get down on the floor?"

"No. Stay where you are. It might attract attention. If there's shooting, get down."

"Okay," surprised at her own calmness.

There were lights shining through the back window now, big lights so you couldn't possibly tell who it was or what kind of car. She looked at him. He always drove with his back straight against the seat, but now he was sitting straighter than a board and driving like a machine. She felt everything drained out of him. He was efficient, emotionless. Down the highway, back into town, and he turned off onto a dirt road near where her car was parked.

"I'll go around once before I come close to your car," he said. They drove, slowly, silently, and now no one was following them. "It's all right now. When we get to the car, you get out, and I'll follow you home just to make sure, and I'll call you in the morning."

"Okay."

The car stopped, and she got out. A man came reeling out of the trees near her, tipped his hat as he went by and went on.

"Get in. He's just a drunken fool," Jason's voice from the car. She got in and drove off.

In the morning, she was doing the breakfast dishes when it occurred to her that one of the decisions she had to make was whether or not she was willing to risk her life for this man. The idea of carrying a gun everywhere was new to her and dangerous. Decisions. Her love for him came up like a wave within her. There were no decisions then. Whatever was necessary, she'd do.

A month before, they'd been talking at T. C.'s, and Jason had said: "You may not want to give all I demand. Or request."

"No," she'd replied, "you don't request, you always demand, and I like it."

So this was part of it, endless miles of dark roads and the dangers that lay along them.

CHAPTER 20

T. C. and the Wilders were evicted within the same week.

"Looks sorta like a conspiracy," Ward Miles said when he heard about it, but they all knew there was nothing to be done.

T. C. was evicted, officially, for eating with white women. In true T. C. fashion, he took on his landlord: "But we been doin' this for years, folks eatin' together, breakin' down the barriers. Won't never get used to it till they seen it done over and over, all them backward people." So he told it to Connie, at least, over coffee at the bus station.

"And what did the landlord say?"

"He said: 'I been watchin' you, T. C., been watchin' an' a reckanin', an' what I seen is what I seen, an' I don' like what I seen.' That man jes' half crazy. He didn' know what to say, but here I am threw out," with a shrug and a smile for the eternal nature of the mess in which they all found themselves. "I tell you, if I thought the nex' worl' wouldn' be no better than this one, I wouldn' wanta go to it."

"What would you do then, keep living?"

T. C. laughed. "Ain't much choice, is there?"

The Wilders were evicted in a ladylike fashion by their landlady, who told them she needed the house for her sister and would be pleased if they'd vacate within a month. They moved quietly. Then the landlady wrote them a letter telling them that they owed her a great deal of money due to damage. Most of the damage she referred to in her letter had been done long before the Wilders had come to Orangedale. Alan wrote back detailing the improvements he had made on the house and explaining that the damage had been done by other people. The landlady called Alan for a conference and withdrew into the vestiges of her Southern ladyhood, exclaiming that she had never had a tenant display displeasure over anything relating to any of her houses and that if he must be so unreasonable then certainly they would forget the whole thing. The Wilders moved into a house ten blocks from where they had been, and the transition was relatively painless. Sometimes, what happened and how you adjusted to it was less important, Connie felt, than the fact that it could still happen, that everything at some level or other was controlled by the notions of race held in the minds of the redneck population and that, despite all their work, they had failed, so far, to make a dent in that control or to substantially alter the nature of the white Southern mind.

A few days after the Wilders moved, Connie and Willie and Robin and Reverend Williams helped T. C. move out to his country place, the place at the end of the road, with the delivery truck. Willie and Robin rode out in T. C.'s pickup truck, and Connie got to ride with Reverend Williams. Against her knee, she held her guitar; she wanted to play at T. C.'s, out in the country, where Jason could hear her.

"Can we hold hands?" she asked.

"When we get out of town. You can't be too careful." He stopped the car for a red light. "There are eight people watching us right now." He hadn't turned his head.

"I know," she said, bitter, thinking how if they were innocent, she might react defiantly now, but since they weren't . . .

"Honey, if anyone knew about us, all your civil-rights work would go up in smoke."

"I know." She sighed, feeling her being diminish. It seemed by some objective standards so terrible. Yet those standards existed at such a distance from the world they inhabited. "If sin is what you want, there must be easier ways to get it."

"But sin is not what we want, and it's not what we've got. What we've got is love, maybe more than we can handle."

They hit the road to T. C.'s stockyard, and he took her hand. It was the first time she'd been down the road in the daytime, and its beauty struck her with new force, backwoods, a feathery tunnel with the sun filtering through the Spanish-moss-clogged trees and onto the ruts and bumps of the road itself, sun staining everything.

"This is the most beautiful place in the world," she said, breathing it in. Arches of trees forming over the road, the road going deeper and deeper into deep Florida, into the nature of her soul.

He smiled. "Let's plan for the next time we see each other before we get out to T. C.'s. No telling who'll be there."

"We can see each other today. . . ."

He put his hand under her skirt and up on her thigh. "I love you, honey. I'd like to wake up some morning and see your sleepy face and kiss your eyes open."

She took his hand again and sighed. Sometimes, sometimes in the middle of their bliss, she saw their situation laid out like a map of pain. "It hurts."

"It hurts to dream, and it's gonna hurt more before we're through."

"Don't."

He looked at her then the way T. C. did sometimes, with the compassion of those who've seen a great deal and lived through it for those who haven't.

"We'll talk about something else then. How's your school coming?"

"Okay. I've got one good course on psychology and literature, on ways of using psychology to criticize literature."

"Ha," he said, "you can't do that. It's no good at all."

"Why not?"

" 'Cause the boys that wrote the books are the ones with the insights, an' if the psychologists had had the insights, they'd have written the books. As it is, all they do is sit around and name the insights. Your course is backwards."

"Well, psychology does have some validity."

"I wouldn't deny that, but it's often wrong, often. And it changes all the time. After all, it rests in the hands of mortals —and mortals who may be less dedicated to the human dilemma than the writers are."

"Or the preachers."

"Could be." He smiled. "Look at Freud, Freud had just one thing on his mind."

"Sex?"

"No, child, reason. That means there're a lot of things going on that he never understood."

"The varieties of religious experience?"

"Yes." Then he turned to her. "You're always surprised when I know anything that comes out of a book, aren't you?"

"A little," she admitted grudgingly.

"They've brainwashed you, honey, all those schools you been to. That's how I got my education, reading; wasn't any other way."

At T. C.'s, Willie and Robin clambered all over the cars. T. C. was carrying pots and books and sparkplugs into a shack similar to the shed at the old place. It was wooden, with an aluminum roof. They went in.

"See, I got two rooms here," T. C. said. "Livin' room and a bedroom." He took them through a break in the wall to where there was a bed and an improvised closet for T. C.'s suits.

"I'm sure you'll make some woman very happy here," Connie said.

"Girl, you gettin' as bad as we are," said Jason. T. C. laughed.

Outside again: "We're African Indians," Willie said. "We're pretty nice to ladies, but we're not so nice to cowboys, 'cause they're always trying to get us."

"Robin's an African Indian too?" Connie asked.

"Yup."

"Then why'd you shoot her?" Robin lay groaning on the ground.

"She was a bad one." He went roaring off, making a noise like an airplane.

"We're about like that," Jason behind her. "We African Indians would as soon shoot down our own as other people."

She got her guitar out of the car and sat down on the steps of the shack to tune it while she listened to them talk.

"We gotta get some kinda voter-registration booth at the barbecue Saturday, a booth where people can make appointments to register," Reverend Williams as he lighted a cigarette.

"Rev here can build the booth," T. C.

"And I'll help him."

"You don't know nuthin' about building."

"No, but I'll be your apprentice, me and my kids."

"Okay. Play something, honey." He and T. C. sat down on rusty chairs and prepared to listen. She sang "If I Had a Hammer," and the song was a passage of memory, and the memory led

to another time she'd sung that song some thirteen years before, the first night she'd seen Alan.

When she'd first gone to college, she'd expected that it
would contain nothing of her New York past; she pictured it as
study and idle sorority and fraternity house parties after football
games for those who chose to partake. Needless to say, she did
not count herself among those people. She wore her ponytail
to college and carried her guitar; she did not expect any of the
Greenwich Village atmosphere to go with her, and she wouldn't
have deluded herself to the point of looking for another Robert
Browning Wallenger.

But then she heard about the folk sings, and now she was
on her way to her first one; her guitar banged comfortably
against her hip, her hair fell long and loose and she wore her
blue jeans and her navy-blue seaman's sweater.

She had to adjust her eyes to the dimness of the candlelight
as she entered the room, for there were candles in red and
green glass globes set at intervals on the floor. There were a
few people there whom she knew well enough to nod to, but
she sat down almost immediately, cross-legged on the floor, and
began to tune her guitar.

"Give me an E," a girl across from her said. As Connie
played it, she felt the note travel across the candle-laden space
and sensed a unity as she and this girl whom she did not know
tuned their guitars together, the sense of unity that seemed to
come to her only from dance and music.

They started singing, more and more people coming and
sitting down with them. The voices rose with the feeling, and
they sang song after song and smoked cigarettes; some people
had glasses of water in front of them to soothe their throats
between songs. She was drinking her glass of water and had just
wiped her mouth on the sleeve of her sweater when she felt
someone watching her. She looked across the lighted circle to see
a strong-looking boy in a white shirt and brown pants lying on
his stomach just looking at her. Good-looking boy, she thought,
too conventionally good-looking for her, a million light-years

away from the exotic, poetic-looking Robert Browning Wallenger. But this boy looked as though he could cut down trees and carry them away while Robert sat and thought about the responsibility and/or necessity of cutting down a tree at all. She went back to her guitar, bending her body over it, strumming it and hitting it rhythmically in preparation for a Spanish song; then later, at the end of the folk sing, "If I Had a Hammer," and all the force of their desire that something better should be made of the world in which they found themselves was in that song. She was aware of the vehemence with which the good-looking lumberjack boy sang the song, and she thought that he was going to ask her out, and longed for the asexual community of the New York folk sings, where no one ever sat around thinking about who they were going to ask out.

But he didn't ask her out for six months. By that time, she was in love with him because her lumberjack image of him had intensified and taken on new dimensions; she liked his sense of purpose, the way he walked, as if he had everything under control. His name was Alan Wilder, and he wanted to be a lawyer. His mind gave her that same impression of control; it ordered things where she saw no order. They conversed casually in a class they took together, and she tried to find out from her friends who knew him how to approach him. One day he came to return a book to her in her dormitory, and she panicked, partly because she'd been sitting in her underwear studying psychology, and she pulled on her navy-blue skirt and her seaman's sweater and crushed her feet into her black loafers and ran downstairs.

He was sitting rigidly at attention in a high-backed chair reading a book in the living room; his hair was cut very short, and when he got up, she realized that he was wearing a navy-blue prep-school blazer, and, looking at him, she thought: Oh God, no! Nothing between us could ever work.

But she forgot these first impressions, especially after he asked her out. They spent a lot of time outdoors, for her impression of him as a lumberjack had been intuitively correct. He came from Maine, and he knew the woods. Eventually, during spring vacation, she was invited to his parents' home. The air was fresh and crisp, and his six brothers and sisters kept her entertained. The house smelled of fresh bread and cookies all the time, and she and Alan took long walks in the woods and came home starving to massive feasts served on the Wilders' long oak table. His world was totally different from hers, and she was enchanted. A year later, they were married.

"That was nice, Connie," Jason pulling her suddenly out of her music and her memories. "Let's go, I gotta see a man at four."

She got up slowly. "Will you drop the kids off, T. C.? I know they want to stay."

T. C. nodded.

"Anytime you want to drop them off," she said, "I'll be home."

In the silent center of the tunnel, he stopped the car and kissed her. "Just remember, whatever happens, I love you."

"Okay. Jason?"

"Mm."

"How many white people have you trusted?"

"One."

"Me?"

"You know it's you. I have so much to teach you. You have to learn to trust the unspoken."

"I know."

"People talk all the time. They say all kinds of things, and you sift them through to try to figure out what they mean. But when people are close, that's different. Can't you just look at me and know what I feel?"

"Sometimes."

"Well, trust it then, honey. It's like that with prayer. The preacher prays aloud, gets the people all worked up an' then they can pray. But the moment of communion, the real moment with God, is silent. Any good preacher has it before he gets to church."

They pulled up in front of her house. "I'll see you at the

meeting tonight and then Saturday morning at the barbecue. Get there early if you're gonna help. Also, I think I got a big comfortable bed lined up for the future."

"Good." She smiled. "You want coffee?"

He looked behind him. "Did you see a laundry truck following us?"

She shook her head.

"Okay."

They went in, and he sat at the dining-room table reading leaflets on the war in Vietnam while she made coffee. When she came in from the kitchen, he'd gotten up and was standing in the middle of the living room.

"He's there all right," he said in his cold, toneless voice. "He's just sittin' there in his truck, watching my car and watching the house."

She came and stood next to him. There was an opening in the closed curtains that they could look through. The orange-and-black truck was parked across the street and around the corner, camouflaged crudely by a single tree.

"Can't wait for coffee. C'mon." He took her hand, and they went back into the dining room, into a corner, and he kissed her good-bye. Always the urgency. "See you tonight at the meeting," and he put on his hat and was gone, like a man walking through walls, and she was left with a pot of coffee boiling on the stove and the unsettled feeling that she was beginning to think of as a permanent part of their relationship.

CHAPTER 21

Driving through an early-morning mist, thick, a mist that might rise or bring rain. There was a big wooden lean-to out at the lot, where they could store the food if it did rain, but the pit was open, and most people would have to eat out in the open. The registration booth would prove hopeless if it rained. Tired. She'd been up until 2:00 A.M. typing letters of protest for the next week.

They pulled onto the dirt road, damp and muddy from the mist and last night's rain, then across another and onto the road that went through the lot itself, the road bumpy and half clotted with weeds, one of the 7,000 roads in the county that weren't paved. She stopped the car, and the children burst out of it while she honked at Reverend Horn, who was standing over the barbecue pit. He waved.

The Reverend Gabriel Horn was one of the best-looking men in town. His face was a record of what he'd been through, and he was bald, which added to the impression of intellectuality that he gave. When he had left his wife, he had staked his girl friends out in different corners of the county so that he could move freely from one to another. T. C. said several women had almost killed him. He'd spent his first eighteen years as a black man in Alabama, and Connie always wondered what he might have become if he had not grown up in America.

She went and stood near him over the large, square barbecue pit. On the grate over it, pots of thick orange sauce boiled, and split chickens and ribs and goat legs were cooking.

"How you doing, Mrs. Wilder?" He was squatting down over the grate, brushing the barbecue sauce onto the meat with a stick wrapped in rags, sweat pouring off his forehead.

"Okay. How're you doing?"

"Hot, tired, but I think we'll have barbecue by ten. Some folks'll wanta eat then."

"Ten? We'll never have the registration booth built by ten. I'm supposed to help Reverend Williams build it. You seen him?"

"Not here yet, probably still in the bed." As he said it, the black-and-white car drew up, Reverend Williams got out and started walking toward them.

"Hey there, Horn, Mrs. Wilder, how you folks doing?"

"You're late," Connie said, hostility her natural mask; she was more conscious now than she ever had been in her life that she was being continually observed, and everything that was beautiful and unimaginably perfect between them became, upon its entrance into the outside world, sordid, dangerous and wrong. She wanted to stand with him in some public place and have him say, We stand together. But it would spell ruin, more kinds of ruin than she could clearly fathom.

"C'mon, girl, we gotta get that booth built." He was staring at her across the pit, staring at her as if he could read her thoughts. They went over to his car to get the lumber.

"What were you thinking about then? You were so deep in it."

She told him, and he sighed.

"It's almost eight o'clock." He shouldered the wood, and they picked their site. Moods. Now he was all carpenter, suddenly absorbed. She watched him, feeling honored to be there. The experience of watching someone totally competent deal in the intricacies of his craft. She began wrenching rusty nails out of the wood with the back of a hammer. The sun broke out of the mist, and the kids played on the grass and ran through the lean-to where the tables were set up.

"What a happy day." She turned to him.

He laughed. "You're such a crazy girl." He took the cigarettes out of his pocket, lighted two and gave one of them to her. "So you're happy now?" he asked, appraising her, watching her with that sense of irony somehow always present.

"Intolerably happy." She could feel her desire rising, she wanted to tear into him. "I couldn't risk my life to go to bed with a man who didn't make me terribly happy."

"Good." He stood up. "Now I'm gonna set the frame up. You come stand here and do what I tell you." She got up and brushed the dirt off her jeans.

Fifty-seven people made appointments to go down to the courthouse and register that day. Reverend Williams worked on the roof of the lean-to making improvements when the booth was finished. He stood on a ladder and hammered, holding the nails in his mouth, spitting them out one by one. She handed him things.

Later, she worked inside the lean-to serving barbecue and baked beans and cole slaw. The children ran up to get money for Cokes and to tell her that Kay Levy was there with her kids. She sat on a log with Kay while Kay ate her dinner. Reverend Williams had gone to a church meeting, and even as she talked with Kay, she was aware of how recently he'd been with her. Kay and Verena were her closest friends, and neither one of them knew, but she couldn't see it fitting into their world views. Verena came up with her two kids, and Kay and Verena sat and talked while Connie went back to serve barbecue. Then T. C. came in from fixing cars and bought a barbecue sandwich and stood retelling the latest gossip while she took orders.

"Connie?"

She looked up and saw Alice. "Yeah?"

"Would you go over to Fontana's and help make some more cole slaw?" She nodded.

A group of boys was playing basketball in one corner of the lot; another was playing baseball in the opposite corner. Knots of people stood eating, some sitting on logs, others in their cars. There were only about three white people there besides herself and Kay, her kids and Kay's kids, but she was growing accustomed to this; there were times when she could almost forget that she was white. She went down the road to Fontana's and up the steps into the small house.

"Hey, Connie." Fontana came out of the bedroom buttoning her blouse. Connie knew there was a man there and felt embarrassed, but Fontana wasn't. She took Connie by the arm into a corner of the room. "Reverend Grey," she whispered, gesturing toward the bedroom. Connie nodded. It wasn't a great surprise to her; T. C. kept her pretty well informed.

"Fawntana," the voice from the bedroom, old voice, Connie thought.

"I came to make some more cole slaw," she said softly, as Fontana started into the bedroom.

Fontana turned around. "Here." She took Connie into the kitchen and gave her the cabbage and a large knife; bunches of carrots were sprayed out across a white-topped table. "I'll help you soon's I get rid of him. Some days he an old pain." She laughed and went out.

Connie started shredding cabbage. There were eight heads of it and four bunches of carrots, all to be cut into a big enamel basin. Reverend Grey. Thinking over what T. C. had said about preachers, and all she'd figured out herself. The preacher was the great, dark father, the dispenser of light and wisdom, the political link with the white community, the purchaser of shoes and meals and the center of love. Since the black community, unlike the white, felt that love implied sensuality, the black preacher was also the sensual center. The difficulty lay in what the preacher did about it. If he had a girl friend, the mothers of the church did all they could to set his wife on his trail and keep her there. If the preacher didn't have a girl friend, the mothers of the church seemed to feel obscurely that he wasn't fulfilling his function, and so they chattered among themselves about that, and some of them wished they could be the one, and others just wished he'd get one so they could begin to intervene. When she'd taken on the Reverend J. H. Williams, she'd taken on the mighty wrath of the mothers of the church, for there was absolutely no provision in the system for the preacher's girl friend being white.

Reverend Grey had chased Fontana, so the story went, till practically all his hair had fallen out, and Fontana, being gracious and not uninfluenced by the fact that the good man had money, had finally given in. Fontana was in no better standing with the mothers of the church than Connie herself, for more hell had been raised by more men at Fontana McClure's than at any other five places in town.

Four heads of cabbage were done when Fontana came back.

"Now," she said, and rolled up her sleeves. She lashed into the cabbage and had a head cut within two minutes. Skill. She had three times Connie's efficiency. She'd waited on tables in white people's homes, served, cooked, cleaned for so many years that every motion was third nature to her. The ancient stereotype had said that black people in the South were lazy.

The truth was not even related to the stereotype. The truth was that they were capable of doing work quickly, efficiently and skillfully, whereas whites often did slow, sloppy jobs and in many cases got away with it.

Fontana took a jar of salad dressing out of the icebox and poured it over the cole slaw.

"Take it on back now," she said.

Connie went out to the dusty road carrying the basin of salad in her hands, the weight, the weight of the weight and the time taken in cutting cabbage and carrots. Once, in the lost hours of a Northern other world, she would have lamented time not spent over her books. Once.

Now the sun was driving downward. It was almost dark, the lot, from a distance, looked cool and the voices sounded different, rich, warm voices—oh, she was a romantic in the most embellished and arcane sense of the word, but people here were so close to what she had been so far from most of her life. The richness of the dark culture. With a feeling of euphoria, she carried the bowl of salad back to the barbecue. His car was there now, and the sun dropping toward the horizon left a deep red glow on the perfect world.

They sat at the edge of the barbecue pit watching the coals die down. The children were still playing, running around, and when they got home, she would toss her easy, natural children into the bed, and they would fall, exhausted, immediately asleep. The natural life. Last year they'd gone to white schools, acquired small new chips on their shoulders and additional middle-class standards; this year they went to black schools and came home enhanced. A sense of spirit and a sense of play. Her image was of the white children propped up on their things—bicycles, wagons, swings and scooters—of the black children creating the world out of their imaginations—dancing so that their bodies grew lithe, singing so that a held spirit kept them in life, whatever happened, until the end.

Reverend Williams was sitting on a stump next to her; she was on the ground. Dressed in his navy-blue suit, impeccable, wearing his hat, he sat by the fire chewing on a goat leg, and she sat next to him with a deep feeling of peace inside her.

"Here." He cut a piece of the meat off with his pocketknife and gave it to her. "You eaten anything today?"

She shook her head and took the meat. Only the murmur of voices around the fire. She ate the meat, and he gave her another piece. Someone on the other side of the fire started singing "We Shall Overcome," and a few people in the distance sang.

He cut another piece of meat off the bone and looked at her, love and sadness in his eyes. "Wednesday night," he said, "nine-thirty."

She nodded and felt herself become real.

CHAPTER 22

The stillness of roads at night. She drove in a series of circles, waiting, watching. In the lighted houses sat people watching TV, talking, eating in a safe space while she drove . . . to the end of the street, around a corner, back down another street, to where they were supposed to meet. He wasn't there yet. The clock in the car said 9:28. Back to the end of the street, down avenues of darkness, quiet, quiet streets, only she was in action, and somewhere he was too, and the rest of the people were sheltered in their houses or cars, unaware that she and Jason were to meet yet strangely involved, because each of them would have had a vested interest in it had they known. She saw a car coming the other way, and as she got close to it, she slowed down ever so slightly. It started to pass.

"Hey," he said.

She parked her car, got out as quickly and silently as she could, opened the door of his car and got in. He drove off.

"Safe," she said and sighed.

"Mm." He was concentrating on the road, on the possibilities, with the same detachment that she'd felt before.

"I feel like a spy," she said.

"No, you probably feel like you're black."

"Maybe so." Stopped briefly for a stop sign. She could feel the tension rise. The trees themselves held dangers and memories of murders. . . . "Being black in the South is like living in the middle of a mined field, isn't it?"

"I wouldn't know. I've never been in a mined field. I imagine it is though."

Off the main road, down a dirt road, vaguely she wondered where they were going, but what mattered was that they were together. He stopped the car by a small house that had only a single outside light. There was a staircase leading up to a small porch where the light shone. A woman came out onto the porch.

"Hey there," she said.

"It's just me," J. H. said.

"Hey, Rev, how you doin'?"

"Fine, Mrs. Charles, how you been?"

"I'm jes' doing fine." She was down the stairs by this time.

"Hey, darlin'," to Connie, "how you doin'?"

"Fine."

Mrs. Charles accepted her without question. Jason had said Mrs. Charles would do anything for him, she was very active in church work; doing anything included this. Now she opened the downstairs door for them.

"There's a hook on the inside of this door and a lock on the bedroom door if you want it. Jes' make yourselves at home, and I'll be upstairs." She smiled and retired. Duenna. Connie kept trying to push her mind far enough open so that it could take in the things she found herself living through. They went in through the laundry room, Jason stopping to hook the door. There was a single blue lightbulb burning outside the bedroom door. They went in and left the door slightly ajar so that the light shone in.

"I don't want to turn the light on in here," he said, "not until we've seen how it goes. If it's okay, then next time we'll turn it on. Can you see?"

"Yes." She watched him take the gun out of his pocket and place it on the bureau. Then he took her in his arms, and she melted into soft fire, their mouths together, the beauty of their one existence, their bodies laden with desire. He put her down on the bed and began undressing her. Their bodies wrapped together, a stillness of the heart, and then . . . she cried when he took her, because his love was powerful and because there was a fountain inside her, and part of that fountain was tears.

Quiet. He was lying on his back looking at her, she on her stomach next to him, braced on her elbows; then she reached out and put her hand on his, and his hand closed over hers, and she felt his touch in her entire being.

He turned on his side. "Come kiss me," and she went, and he held her, kissing her open throat and her breasts. Slow, with the full desire coming on her again and again. She didn't exist except through him.

"You scare me," she said.

"Why?" He looked at her.

"So much love."

"It's not me, it's us. We scare me too." His hand pushing

146

the hair back from her neck, his hands on her breasts arousing her, he growing big with his love for her and taking her so that they sank into a single motion inside a volcano. She couldn't believe that anyone could get that far into her, take her so completely, leave her so limp. They were bound, loving, one flesh, one spirit.

Now he said, "We've got to go, darlin'," and as he tried to pull himself out of her, they turned, falling into a new way of being together rather than becoming separate, and she felt the electrical charge of him within her, and his power, and she didn't think anything could ever touch them, ever pull them apart, because they were one person. "Oh, baby, I'd like to stay inside you forever."

"I'd like you to," with the deep wonder always at their being one, as if they'd passed through one another so completely that they were intermixed.

"We've got to go." He got up and started dressing. She was still lying there. "Come on, darlin', I gotta get home. It's after one."

She sat up and swung her legs onto the floor. Home, he said it so easily, and it made her shudder; the word said he'd done this before, that he knew the pattern, while for her . . . She looked around the small, dimly lit room that she'd never been in before tonight. "Home," she said as she sat there hooking her bra.

He fastened his belt and looked down at her with such love that she felt even his look was enough; if there'd been nothing else, his look would have been enough. "My real home is here," he said, "in this room, with you. And whatever happens, it always will be."

She got off the bed then and dressed, but the tears were running down her face.

"Don't cry, baby, I only want you to cry 'cause you're happy."

She smiled. "I *am* happy," she said. "I'm happy and unhappy and open."

He put his hat on. "You ready?"

She nodded.

"I'll go out first and check, and then I'll signal." He went out and in a moment was at the door again. She turned the light off and followed him out. He closed the door, and she got into the car.

Off the dirt road and on the highway again, and he was absolutely alert, so she didn't say anything. She was learning when to be silent. Masses of trees passed in the darkness, an occasional streetlight, the dark, open road, wonderful because in some strange way it was their home, that dark pathway ahead, the pathway from their bedroom into an outside world where what they did when they were alone was completely hidden.

"That man in front of us disappeared," he said. "He just cut his lights. Must be parked somewhere." She picked the gun up off the floor and put it on the seat next to him. He swerved left at the next crossroad. We'll take a detour and get out of his way." They drove half a mile and turned down a dirt road. They were close to her car now.

"I didn't know it could feel that good," she said.

"But it does."

"When am I going to see you again?"

"Why don't you come to my church in the country Sunday?"

"Okay. How do I get there?"

"I'll call you in the mornin' and tell you." He reached over and opened the car door for her, and she got out. "Sleep good, darlin'."

"I will."

Flowers were blossoming inside her, and she could shake them out of her hair. A sense of peace somewhere inside, a sense of completion. If someone had told her that the next time she went to bed with him she would disappear into him and never be heard from again, she would still have rushed to him.

Driving, always driving down a dark tunnel filled with love. The streetlights gleamed it, the road was what he traversed, his roads, her roads, the imprint of their tires like footprints, with the dark, brilliant Florida sky overhead. She drove back into time.

CHAPTER 23

They drove to the country. He had two churches, and one was in the country. This was the church he'd built with his own hands. They drove through miles of fields; in the spring, the fields would be full of cucumbers, and beyond the cucumber fields were the tobacco fields. Finally they drove down a dirt road suddenly crowded with cars going to his church. She pulled off the road and parked.

"How long will it be?" Willie asked, pulling at his collar.

"Long probably." She sighed. "So just stop thinking about it, and we'll get a treat after if you're good." Robin pulled her socks up from where they'd slipped down into her shoes. "Now please stand up and behave."

The church was white, wooden, and the roof on the square steeple was blue, all of it done with craftsmanship. She wondered at him, deeply and continuously. He had built a church with his own hands, and he stood inside it and preached, something so simple, so clear-cut and so completely removed from anything that had been her life.

They went in. Inside, the church smelled of new wood, and the windows were light-blue glass, as if pieces of the sky had been cut out and shoved into the church. At the front of the church was a raised dais and the pulpit. On the dais was a row of chairs, and he sat in one of them, proud and detached and burning with a God-given fire, as if, before he came into the church, he had emptied out his soul, so that it could be filled with light, so that when he preached, he would radiate light all over the church. Behind the dais was the choir stall, three more rows of chairs; his wife was in the choir, and at the left of the choir stall was a piano, and a girl in a yellow dress sat playing it.

Then he got up. The power and the glory and the majesty. All at once, with all that light burning in him, she had the sensation that maybe after all he was God and that all the rest of it was a sham, for he'd said that people regarded him as if he were a god, and this was what he'd meant. She hadn't imagined for a single instant when he'd said it that it could be anything like this.

"This morning I'm going to read the text from the scriptures that I'm going to preach from later. I don't usually do this, but today is homecomin', and I want to keep that theme in mind all the time we're here. The text starts with the 38th verse of the 23rd chapter of Matthew:

Behold, your house is left unto you desolate.
For I say unto you, Ye shall not see
me henceforth, till ye shall say, Blessed
is he that cometh in the name of the Lord.

This is our theme today: What does homecoming mean? Jesus said: 'I have gathered thy children together, even as a hen gathereth her chickens under *her* wings, and ye would not!' This is what the church tries to do, to take everyone in before it's too late, but do the people come? No. It's just as Jesus says: 'And ye would not.'

"Thass right," from the pew in front of Connie.

"People refuse comfort when it's offered and then suddenly wonder why they're comfortless and uncomfortable. One of the paradoxes of human behavior is that people refuse what they most want and need. A man doin' some farming, an' someone offers him some help. 'I don't need no help,' he says, an' the other man goes away. Then next thing you hear is this man who was offered some help groanin' away about how he got to do all the work on his lan' and has no help. There's no sense in that, so remember, when someone tries to gather you in or help you, don't refuse him but accept, the more you accept, the more your heart will open." He closed his big Bible and turned and walked off the dais. He was wearing his dark-blue suit, and he looked large and square. He went out a door at the front of the church and disappeared.

Robin squirmed, and Connie whispered to her to hold still. Willie sighed, loosened his tie but seemed more absorbed; Connie watched the women, the rhythms of women in church; people already seemed calmer than they had at the beginning of the service, the power of his word . . .

Then the syncopated piano began, and before the music had settled into her, there came the sound of singing, as if

from some other world, soft at first and then growing from a
voice that carried the seeds of extraordinary beauty:

Jesus is my Saviour
Wholly by my side
I know that He will guide me
Know that He will love me
Even when I stray....

The song filled the small church, beat against the pieces of
sky that served as windows and soared beyond, and Connie
watched the woman who sang, caught and held in the act of
creation. The woman in front of her was crying, weeping uncontrollably, bending over and rocking back and forth, keening,
the age-old release in tears, and the woman next to her
put her arm around her.

Then there was silence in the church, and a slender bald-
headed man the color of mahogany rose from the preacher's
corner and came over to the table that sat on the floor in
front of the dais. He got down on his knees and faced the
pews, his hands clasped on top of the table, gnarled, tired,
praying hands:

Oh Lord
We are humble in Thy sight
And we ask forgiveness....

First he spoke it through, mumbling almost, fast, for everyone
knew it; then he did the first line slowly, and everyone joined
in, chanting and singing and humming so that the sound
rose and fell like sea water, and the woman in front of Connie
began thumping her heel against the floor in time to the chanting, and someone else at the back of the church began clapping
rapidly with a sudden staccato beat, and when it was over,
the man got up painfully from the floor and returned to his
seat. Reverend Williams came in again, creating a hushed
air of expectancy. He came to the pulpit and raised his arms
in blessing: "Dear Heavenly Father, we pray today that you
show us the meaning of this homecoming day and that you
open our hearts so that we can receive the gifts your son

gave us, bless the afflicted, give strength to the weak, and make the strong generous and humble. In Jesus' name, Amen." The music rising as he sat down. The choir stood and sang, and the song was picked up by the people in the pews.

Then the sermon. He got up and came to them and looked out over the congregation before he spoke, the fire of all his ancestors burning in his eyes:

O Jerusalem, Jerusalem thou that killest the prophets, and stonest them which are sent unto thee, how often would I have gathered thy children together, even as a hen gathereth her chickens under her wings, and ye would not!

Behold your house is left unto you desolate.

For I say unto you, Ye shall not see me henceforth, till ye shall say, Blessed is he that cometh in the name of the Lord.

He recited it from memory, and then he waited, as if to see whether everyone had absorbed it.

"By the 'house' in our text we are, I think, to understand the temple in which these words were spoken. It had ceased to be inhabited by sincerity. The piety that had built it and which it had once enshrined had become a perished thing. Its gorgeous ritual, its priesthood, its sacrifices no longer stood for reality, and therefore, instead of being an embodiment of spiritual truth, were a living lie, as hurtful to man as they were hateful to God.

"Once religion degenerates into mere formalism, it reacts on its votaries with disastrous results. Better no profession of faith at all than one which is empty. The peril of all religions is that the forms which they build up for the expression of life become their means of sterilization.

"When religion divorces itself from morality, every kind of fraud becomes possible. The old proverb says, 'The corruption of the best is the worst of corruption.' The temple is the corporate expression of a people's belief in God and things unseen. When it ceases to express the spirit of worship and truth, it brings but darkness and death. When behavior has broken with belief, then the house of God becomes simply a last year's nest from which the spirit bird has taken wing."

"Amen, amen, amen." It was Mrs. Sims. The wing of the spirit bird had caught her, and all that quietness flowed out of her small, thin body, and she was taking off. Mrs. Sims, in a bright-green hat with a veil and a green dress, stood up, put both her arms straight up in the air, began stamping one foot rhythmically and shouting hard, sheer, regular cries. The woman next to Mrs. Sims tried to control her, and the woman they called Big Mama in the pew in front of her said "Hallelujah" and clapped her hands.

Finally Mrs. Sims sat down, and everyone looked back at Jason.

"Nothing can be more drear or depressing than an empty house. Israel's house was left desolate in order that it might awaken old memories and beget a desire to return. The discipline of loneliness was not an end but a means to an end. There is always a purpose behind the chastisement of God.

"The ritual may still have been beautiful, but without sincerity, it becomes the corporate negation of religion. For the temple of stone is merely the formal expression of the temple within the heart. The temple of Christ's time had cut itself off from the divine source of spiritual energy. Even its acquired momentum had slowed down. The wheels of the machine were now turned by hand.

"And what hands! They were the avaricious hands of priestly parasites whose palms were ever itching for bribes, of ecclesiastical mercenaries who exploited the religious instincts of the people for private or personal ends, and the men," and he began singing it, "like the men of today, preying on the needs of the poor, promising them heaven and cheating them out of earth . . . ," preaching and singing, carrying everyone with him, and Mrs. Sims was up again:

"Yes, yes, oh yes Lord."

And the woman in front of Connie was crying again, and Connie looked at Jason and saw the tears in his eyes; it was like watching a mountain split.

Finally church was over, but not without Jason making it clear that they should be back to church by three and again that night, for, after all, they had nothing to do that day but attend church and worship the Lord. Connie had such a feeling of peace all through her that she felt there was nothing she would have liked better than to spend the whole day and half the night in church.

Outside, Willie and Robin ran around with some of the other children, and T. C. and Reverend Horn arrived from another church for the later service, and the sky was bright blue and open, and the trees so green against it that she felt she might burst.

She stood with Horn and T. C. talking about the service and the weather, and then he came up.

"Hello, Mrs. Wilder, how'd you enjoy the service?"

"I enjoyed it." There was an explosion of feeling within her, and she felt the necessity of keeping it down. "It was a good performance." That was the kind of remark they all expected from her. His wife came up and put her arm through his, binding him to her.

"You hear what that girl said." He turned to his wife. "She said it was a good performance. That girl's crazy."

They both laughed.

"Mrs. Wilder, have you met my wife?"

She shook her head, not trusting her voice.

"Mrs. Wilder, my wife, Mrs. Williams."

They shook hands. "You better stay to dinner, Mrs. Wilder"— Jason smiled as he said it—"and give those children of yours some soul food."

Before she could sort out her thoughts to decide what she ought to say, another voice seconded the invitation: "Yes, do." It was a woman's voice, warm and confident, solid and rich like the earth. It was the soloist.

"Have you met Mrs. Holmes?" Mrs. Williams. And another introduction, so much of his world that she didn't know.

"I'll have to call my husband if we're going to stay for dinner."

"You can call from my house." Mrs. Holmes gestured across the road. They walked slowly across; Connie felt in awe of this woman and therefore found it difficult to speak.

"I'd say something about your singing," she said finally, "but I don't think there are any words to express it."

"Because it was so good or bad?" Mrs. Holmes was smiling.

"*Good.* You mean you really don't know how good it is?"

Mrs. Holmes shrugged. "You never really know, do you? You're always only yourself judging it. Sometimes I think I judge it right, and sometimes I think I judge it wrong, but I never *know.*"

"That's true," Connie said, thinking she didn't really know how well she danced.

Mrs. Holmes pushed open a screen door, and they went across a white porch that had plants all across shelves at either end of it, then into a living room.

"How many children do you have?" she asked Mrs. Holmes.

"Six," and she smiled.

"Six?"

"How many do you have?"

"Just those two you saw running around at the church."

"You going to have more?"

Her hand was already on the phone, her finger in the hole to dial, but she stopped. "I don't know. My husband wants more, but I don't think I do." She hadn't told that to anyone, and she wondered now what had possessed her, with a woman she'd met five minutes ago, but she looked at Mrs. Holmes' face and knew that the information was safe. More children. Good lord, no, not now.

"Can we stay for dinner at the church?" she asked Alan.

"I've had a sandwich, and I'm about to go to the law school. Would it make any difference to you these days if I said you couldn't stay?" his voice taut.

"I don't know, yes, of course it would."

He sighed deeply. "Well, it doesn't matter. What time is dinner here tonight?"

"Seven?"

"All right. See you then," and he hung up.

"Bye," she said into the phone.

As they started back across the road, Mrs. Holmes put her hand on her arm. "Look," she said, "I don't know if I should say this, but I've heard about your civil-rights work and your dance group, and those of us who know what's going on in town are with you, but some of these people here, they're country people, and if some of them are a little hostile . . . " She looked at Connie.

"They're not used to seeing white people in their church," she finished for her.

Mrs. Holmes nodded.

Laughter came from the churchyard, and some people had driven off down the dirt road. Now others were beginning to file into the gray wooden shed where they were going to have dinner.

"We eating here?" Willie came up to her.

"Yes."

"Good. I'm starved. I could eat a rattlesnake."

They followed Mrs. Holmes into the building. On one table the food was laid out: platters of fried chicken and pork chops and barbecued ribs and ham, bowls of black-eyed peas and ham hocks, okra and tomatoes, sweet potatoes and plates of corn bread and hush puppies. Mrs. Holmes handed her a plate, and she began serving herself.

"C'mon, Mrs. Wilder, bring your food over before it gets cold," the same sense she'd had the day she met him that she was being ordered to do something and that she'd obey without question.

She sat down at the big table. It was long, like a picnic table, and there were benches on either side of it. He sat on a chair at the end of the table and presided. She sat on a bench opposite his wife, with Horn on one side of her and T. C. on the other, the two of them flanking her like bodyguards. Mrs. Holmes sat down next to Mrs. Williams, and two older women who watched her hostilely, with only slightly veiled dislike, replenished plates.

She ate silently for a few minutes, waiting for something to be said. Jason sat at the end of the table, buttering his bread, cutting his meat, eating as if he either didn't know or couldn't care less that his wife and his mistress sat opposite each other at his table.

156

"Hey, Horn, what did Reverend Sanders preach on?" Jason spoke, barely looking up from his food.

"Marriage," Horn said. "Said some inspiring things."

"I think I might get married again," T. C. said, holding a huge forkful of black-eyed peas inches above his plate, "just so's I can get me some sweet tater pie like I see over on that table."

"I made the pie," Mrs. Holmes said, "and you can have as much of it as you want without marrying me." Everyone laughed.

"But if you should marry Mrs. Holmes, you'd get a wife with a voice too," Jason said. "She could sing you to sleep at night."

"I'd like that," Reverend Horn said, looking appreciatively at Mrs. Holmes.

"And you'd get six children too," Connie added.

"Couldn' do that," Horn mused. "Got four right now."

"But your wife would have those."

"My wife ain't getting those children." Everyone laughed again, but Horn was serious. "Matter of fact, I might go back to my wife."

"Reverend Sanders inspire you to do that?" Jason was scrutinizing Horn now.

"Maybe so."

"You still haven't told us what he *said*," Jason growing impatient.

"His text was 'As the church is subject unto Christ, so let the wives be to their own husbands in everything.' "

"Christ should be at the center of every marriage," Mrs. Williams.

Connie worked at cutting her pork chop into tiny pieces; the whole discussion was becoming unbearable.

"Yes, yes," Horn said, "Christ and the church at the center of marriage and a bond of union between man and wife entered into in God's name."

Connie turned to look at Horn, but his face was blank. Horn and his women. Yet what was going on in his head was infinitely subtler and more complicated than hypocrisy. Hypocrisy was basically a white middle-class game; this game had to do with the multiple secrets of survival, with the necessity of manhood established by conquest, by love and the use of a gun rather than by status and money.

"I'm ready for my pie now, Mrs. Holmes." T. C. handed her his plate and wiped his mouth on his napkin. "Yep, I sure do think I'll get married for sweet potata pie."

"That's a lousy reason to get married, T. C.," Connie.

"It certainly is." Mrs. Williams nodded her head in agreement.

"Marriage is the foundation of family, and family is the foundation of society." Horn was off again. "And anyone breakin' the bonds of the family breaks the bonds of society. . . ."

"T. C.'s not so far wrong." Jason pushed his plate back and lighted a cigarette. "Woman's got to know how to cook. Can you cook, Mrs. Wilder?" It was the last thing she was ready for.

"Yes," she said, looking him dead in the eye, "I can cook."

"You know the way we was raised around here, black people doing most of the cooking for whites." Why was he doing this? And he *knew* she could cook; it was all part of the cover, but she felt resentful. She could feel the hostility of the women serving them, almost touch it, their eyes boring into her back.

"Well, it isn't that way all over. I started cooking when I was eight years old, and nobody ever did our cooking for us." She glanced up and caught a look of real surprise on one of the women's faces. So even that remark he'd planned, constantly teaching.

"Cooking isn't that important," Mrs. Williams said. "What's important is forgiveness. That's what binds a marriage together, holds it tight as anything. Whatever a person does in marriage, the other person has to forgive him and forget about it, just forgive and forget, no matter how many times it has to happen." Her voice had a hard edge to it, and this time Connie had to look at her because she knew she was being stared at directly, and she couldn't avoid the confrontation.

"Yes, I suppose that is important," she said, trying to control the tone of her voice, "but I don't think that's all of it." Giving, the voice inside of her said, love, honor and obey and give, give until you don't know where one of you ends and the other begins.

Jason sat at the end of the table, smoking imperturbably, watching them, the king with all his subjects around him.

"Time to go." He stood up. "Church begins again in fifteen minutes."

They all stood up, and she helped Mrs. Holmes clean up, which seemed to confuse and somewhat distress the two older ladies. Mrs. Holmes sent them back to church. "You see what I mean," she said.

"Yes, but you've got to get used to it," Connie said. "If there's ever going to be any real integration, all this has to be gone through."

"You're very serious about things, aren't you?" Mrs. Holmes was looking at her.

"Yes," Connie said, wondering if there was something wrong with that.

"It's okay." Mrs. Holmes laughed. "I am too."

They went outside.

"Are we going to church *again*?" Willie came racing up.

"No." She laughed. "But a lot of people are."

"Come out and see us," Mrs. Holmes said, "now that you know where we live."

"Thanks, I will," and they climbed into the car and waved to Mrs. Holmes, and, as she started the motor, Connie watched her go into the church, and she could hear them starting to sing in the church. She could imagine Jason sitting on a chair, tired and full and imperturbable, only the beginnings of his holy fire there. As she drove off, she felt her pain beginning, the pain that filled her when she wanted to be with him for always and knew that she couldn't be, ever.

CHAPTER 24

The road to T. C.'s was the road to freedom, and the road to Mrs. Charles' was the road to pleasure. On a clear, cold evening in December, with a moon burning above, she drove toward Mrs. Charles', parked on their street, and he picked her up.

"We're leaving in two days for Berkeley," she said.

"For how long?"

"Three weeks."

"I'll miss you."

"I'll miss you too, and I don't miss people."

"I know." He laughed. "You're so tough." His laughter was like his love, taking her over, making her place in the world.

He pulled up next to Mrs. Charles' small house and cut the car lights. Mrs. Charles stood, a dark silhouette, against her lighted doorway.

"I think we should go up and see her," Connie said.

"She'd like that."

"But just for a minute."

He smiled.

When they reached the top of the stairs, Mrs. Charles put her arm around her. "Hey there, darlin', how you doin'?"

"Fine. How are you?"

"Jes' fine."

The three of them went into Mrs. Charles' room.

"Sit down," Mrs. Charles said, "sit down."

Jason sat in a large armchair facing Mrs. Charles' dressing table, and Connie sat on a couch. Mrs. Charles had on a white dressing gown, worn silk, and the lapels lay open, revealing her thin, dark neck. As she talked, she pushed strands of her hair into an untidy bun that lay on her neck.

"Y'all be welcome to come anytime at all, an' I'll jes' keep the place ready. There's a heater down there so's it won't get too cold. . . ." She talked on, as easy in the situation as Connie was uneasy. "Joe come up here, an' he get all worried 'bout someone comin', an' he tell me I'm more than half crazy lettin' y'all come here, but I tell him, it's Rev, honey, an' you oughta be willin' to go out on a lotta limbs for a man like that."

"What'd Joe say?" Jason laughed.

"He say: 'Reckon so, but ain't a lotta good you can do no one after you been shot.'"

"That boy's the one's crazy. Ain't nobody gonna get shot."

Connie looked at her hands. He always prepared himself for the worst, but that didn't mean that realistically he thought it was going to happen. To think like Joe thought was paranoia, to go anywhere without a gun was downright ignorance.

"We better be goin', Mrs. Charles. We'll see ya."

"Thank you," Connie said, and Mrs. Charles smiled and pressed her hand. Casually they left, as if they'd been invited for coffee or dinner. She felt her consciousness constantly being pushed beyond the limits she'd known, then resisting, then going still further. The unknown existent. In the puritan culture in which she'd grown up, sex was confined to books, to people's bedrooms and to innuendo. Here, people were generous on religious principle. Mrs. Charles regarded their situation casually because she was helping out a man she respected, that was all. Connie felt herself being weaned away from the puritans.

Down the stairs. Into the outer room, through to their room. He snapped on the light.

"Look," he said. She turned. She'd been unbuttoning her dress. On the bed between the pillows lay a big plush Santa Claus with a foolish smile on his face. They looked at each other, smiled, and then she felt their pain pass between them. He took her in his arms, and she felt tears on her face.

"Stop," he said. He put his hands inside her dress. "I love you, more than I've ever loved another human being. Whatever happens to us, remember that."

"Don't say whatever happens, don't say it."

"Oh, child," love answering love always. He took the Santa off the bed and turned it face down on the bureau. "Don't want no Santa watching us." He pulled her to him again. "I haven't bought your gift yet. No money."

"I haven't bought yours either. I'm going to buy it in Berkeley or San Francisco."

"Good."

In their kiss she felt the beginning of the bond forming, his hands on her breasts, his eyes watching her face for the change, the desire rising. She brushed her silent hair across his face, her ache to become his, as always, tremendous, and what happened then was beyond what she'd known, what was in her of him fusing them, filling her with his warmth, blinding her, making her pass through some spasm of ecstasy and then be wholly quiet as she lay in his arms, her head on his chest, his hand stroking her hair.

"I belong to you," she said softly, "and I've never belonged to anyone before, never."

"Darlin', I could never get enough of you."

"If we got married, we wouldn't wear any clothes for a week."

"That's a honeymoon." He pulled her against him.

Love was a subtle blending of spirits. She could not believe how warmly they became one, as if their skin were gone and all the nerves in her body were connected to all the nerves in his so that they felt everything together. Deep in the slowness of their love, laughter at her hair in his mouth, kissing him, kissing his mustache, out of that slowness she spoke:

"You're all I know of God."

"You've got to learn more. That's not enough for you to live by."

"I've got a theory that God for a woman is always a man, and if she believes enough in him, the way I believe in you, she'll do anything he asks. God for a man is an ego projection. Each man's God is just a big him thinking like him. Women live for men, and men live for themselves."

"You're a primitive," he said. "Religion is much more so-phisticated and logical than you make it. C'mon, we gotta go home."

"All right," sighing. He always started dressing first. "Some-day, I'm gonna leave you in bed while I go make breakfast."

"I hope so, baby," an allusion to something they'd never allowed themselves to discuss. "I hope so, but I don't think so."

Her clothes seemed to her awkward, uncomfortable. She wanted to be lying naked in his arms again. Love was a bond of pain.

Driving through a cool, dark night. For once, no danger perceived, only suspected. He held her hand all the way to the car.

He turned the motor off and put her hand to his lips. "Remember, I love you. Remember that when you're in Berkeley and San Francisco. Whenever it is and wherever it is, we'll be together again," his words falling into her heart always as if they promised a final parting.

"Good night, my love."

"Good night, darlin'."

She got out of his car, alone, and into her car and drove off enclosed in its shell, protected from the cool wind-swept darkness outside.

CHAPTER 25

It was three weeks of conflict, her two worlds joining momentarily, then bouncing off each other. It was confusing to her because people she loved saw things from radically different perspectives. Her world now was Orangedale, but she could not communicate to people in Berkeley and San Francisco the wisdom she had gained there.

Now she was back, it was night and she was without a car, walking across the dark town. While she'd been in Berkeley, four black men had been jumped in Uncle Jim's Pancake Shack, the local KKK hangout. Now there were rumbles of action, and she was on her way to a meeting of the FTA where someone from out of town was going to give training in nonviolence.

She turned off the paved streets onto the dirt road, and the atmosphere changed, as if a curtain had fallen. The road wound under the trees, and she walked past a juke where men sat at square tables and played cards and drank beer. A large, lighted square of window on the dark road. Passing it, forbidden as it was, forbidden as it all was to her, she felt like a child entering the adult world through the back door.

The church shone light, and a man's voice, angry, haranguing, echoed out onto the road. As she went into the church, she felt her heart open. She hadn't seen Jason in nearly a month, and she missed him almost as if she was missing a part of herself.

Crowds of people were in the church: the black community out in force, older people from the League, students from the university in boots and black pants, students who worked with the FTA when it seemed to them part of the movement. The man talking was tall and dark and had a wild bush of black hair. She didn't know him, but there was something familiar about him. She sat down next to Alice.

"Hey, sugah, how you doin'?" the reassurance of Alice's warmth.

"Okay, you?"

"Jes' fine."

"Who *is* that up there?"

"That's Johnnie McClure, Fontana's bigges' boy. He's one of the boys got beat up in the pancake shack." It was the McClure resemblance she'd detected, the same eyes and bone structure.

"So this cat come up behin' me an' say: 'What you doin' here, boy?' An' I tells him: 'Jes drinkin' coffee, ol' man, mindin' my own business.' An' he go on, 'What you call me, boy?' An' I turn slowly on my seat an' look in his ugly ol' face an say: 'Man, if I'm a boy, then you a old old man.' Then someone flip the lights, an' nex' thing I know, I'm into a big fight, hitting right and left, eight men on top of me. An' then someone hit me with a blackjack an' they toss me out an' I'm groggy, but I know Joey, he still in there, an' he a kid can't half throw a punch, so back I go and get in a few punches 'fore they toss me out again. But this time we all out on the sidewalk, an' we get up, an' I say to Joey: 'Man, we gotta go to the po-lice.' An' Joey, he say: 'No, ain't no use in that.' But I tells him, 'Man, po-lice supposed to protect our interest.' So I drags him down there, an' the po-lice didn' want no part of our warrant. But we got some white reinforcements, went down again, but that was ten days ago, an' we ain't had no action. Now I'm tellin' you the time has come for us to take action ourselves. Wait for the white man to do it, might as well wait for the day of judgment itself, an' I know that's what a lotta you is doin', but it ain't comin' soon, even preachers'll tell you that. So what're we gonna do now? That's all I'm axing; you think it's okay for any black man to get beat up every time he wanta cup of coffee, that okay?"

"No," came the response, "that ain't right. Been going on too long now."

"'Bout half of what he says is true," Alice said to Connie. "Can't hardly trust a McClure."

"So now we goin' in there, black and white alike, an' we gonna show 'em that we can have coffee wherever we like, ain't nobody gonna stop us. But we ain't gonna fight 'em, we goin' in nonviolent," with his fists clenched and his chest tightening. "Here's Ted Davis."

A square-built, strong-looking, light-skinned man got up. "Nonviolent training," he said, "can be rough, so I hope you're dressed for it. In this sort of situation, girls shouldn't wear high heels. If you've got long hair, put it up; they'll grab for your hair first. If you've got pierced ears, don't wear earrings; they may rip your ears open if they can get something to hang onto. Always protect what's most vulnerable. Girls, protect your breasts. Guys, you know what to protect. Dress decently when you're sitting in or picketing. The crazier you look, the less people will have to come to terms with your ideas. Now this is the nonviolent position," and he crouched down, the style of his motion almost revealing the situation that would demand the action. He locked his hands across his skull; then he rolled rapidly over and jumped to his feet. "Now if a guy near you is being kicked, you can't kick the guy who's doing the kicking. The best you can do is throw your body over your buddy's body. C'mere, Joey."

Joey, slender and obliging, came up.

"Now get in the nonviolent position."

Joey crouched. Ted threw himself down over Joey.

"Hey, man, I'd rather be kicked," Joey's muffled voice, and there was laughter in the church, an easing of spirit. Connie could feel the tension in her chest. They all lived under continual pressure, wishing for and fearing confrontation, and this would be it. . . . They were going straight into the enemy's lair.

"Now," Ted went on, "we'll have some run-throughs. C'mon, volunteers, two girls, two guys."

Connie raised her hand, eager to get into it.

The run-throughs were a farce, laughter and horsing around, masking a grim reality. The boys knocked each other with their shoulders and feigned aggression, doing parodies of rednecks with exaggerated leers and slumps. Connie was marching across the platform, bumping into people, filled with laughter, glad to be home, when she suddenly turned, as if her eyes were drawn by a magnet, to the back of the church, and there he stood, dressed up, in his immaculate dark suit and light topcoat, in marked contrast to the kids in their jeans and rough shirts, and she yearned to be with him, standing next to him, dressed up, and part of his world. . . .

CHAPTER 26

On the eighth of January, they began sitting in at Uncle Jim's Pancake Shack, and Connie went every night at ten, carrying her Latin books or John Donne so that her school schedule wouldn't fall completely apart. During the day, they picketed in front of the place and handed out leaflets to passers-by. At night, the cops began to patrol, waiting for trouble, their cars nervously poised at intervals along the street, and T. C., deputed by a committee consisting of himself, Jason H. Williams and Gabriel Horn, circled the Pancake Shack all night long.

On January 10, Johnnie McClure and a white couple named Winters who'd done a lot of work in the movement were arrested for contributing to the delinquency of a minor; a young boy on probation from the reform school had lied about his age, sat in and stayed at several people's houses. The laws about such things were vague in outline and worded loosely enough to encompass whatever group of people the reigning magistrates wished them to.

At four that afternoon, Connie arrived at the Winters'. At least twenty people were already there. The long table in the dining room was the center; ashtrays filled with butts and half-filled cups of cold coffee were laid at various points on the table like a map of the time passed meeting there. Two people were frantically typing at the table; three men sat conferring over thick piles of paper and lawbooks. In the living room, people were kneeling on the floor making demonstration signs with laundry markers. Jason came in, and they sat beside each other for a little while and talked, drinking cups of warmed-over coffee; and she wished they could find some obscure corner where he could take her in his arms and reassure her. He was handling the Human Rights Commission angle on the sit-ins, and he left her and moved from group to group, smoking and consulting. Ward Miles came in with some other people from the FTA, and T. C. came in with news from the rednecks, which he somehow always managed to obtain while working at various jobs, fixing people's cars, drinking coffee at the bus station, providing a listening ear and an open heart.

"Now, we're marching tonight"—Ward got up—"from the AME church on the north side down to the jail. We'll carry

169

signs and sing, and it'll all be very orderly. Got it?" Choruses of response.

At eight that night, there was a meeting at the AME church. She went in and was struck by the white faces sprinkled among the dark, by the white arms along the backs of pews. The kids from the university entered and left the black community as if they were· all hitched to a single string. Only she and the Winters and a few others went regularly into the churches, emblematic of the situation, of its intensity and difficulty. They were the white tokens dropped into the collection plate.

The meeting was brief, the church charged with everyone's tension. If Johnnie McClure was not popular in the black community, and he wasn't, he had hit the right chords this time, and his past had been momentarily forgotten. The Winters were popular, and people's general response was compounded by the fact that they were involved.

The march was to wind down to the jail, and Johnnie and the Winters were due to be released on bail at about the time the march arrived. There would be singing and a certain amount of publicity, and an occasion for some fear and more tension would be transmuted into an occasion for joy.

She took her place in line, shouldered a sign that read, "Johnnie McClure's Only Crime Is Being Black," and the march began. . . . They sang as they marched down the sidewalks, across streets, two cops on motorcycles riding at a distance from them, their leaders shepherding them across streets, a beautiful black girl leading the singing, her voice rising above the rest, walking beside her husband, a slender white boy.

The march went by the large darkened mass of the Court-house, in itself an object to be protested, the citadel of the white, the safe, the moneyed.

Down the dark street, onto the dirt road that led to the paved area that led to the county jail. . . . They marched, and there was a feeling of elation, a sense of convictions felt, sustained and expressed so that they became tangible and translated for other people, who reacted with fear or awe.

They stood before the jail; Johnnie and the Winters were brought out, and stood on the steps in front of the lighted panels of doors that led into the jail. Ellie Winters was crying, Johnnie clasped his hands over his head in a gesture of victory and one of the student leaders made a speech. Then they stood massed around the doors of the jail, closing in on Johnnie and the Winters, hugging them, talking, feeling the bonds form, and the police watched them from inside the jail, uniformed, in control and obviously uncomfortable. The TV cameras rolled, the newsmen wandered in the crowd, the man from the local radio station offered Johnnie a microphone, and Connie had the impression that it was a carefully staged performance until Ward and Vanessa, almost at the same moment, began singing "Before I'll Be a Slave." . . .

And the memory of a story of Jason's came to her. When he'd been a child, his father had farmed on a small plot of land, but the land had been part of the big land, and the white man's house had been only up the hill, the master's house, for his father had been born a slave. And Jason said that when the white man had called his father, his father had gone, in one swift involuntary motion, and that even when his father had been eating, he'd spit the food out of his mouth to answer the white man's call. And Jason had sworn that he'd never do anything like that for any man as long as he lived, even if it meant his life. And he hadn't. His great fear had always been that he'd kill a man. And they sang again. . . . And it struck her how it was a matter of life and death to all of them and only a matter of choice for her and others like her. They played at civil rights as they played at life, and promised nothing permanent of themselves and sacrificed nothing permanent of themselves. Yet, for the first time in her life, she wasn't just playing, and the knowledge struck a stone-cold note to the heart.

CHAPTER 27

The arrest of Johnnie McClure and the Winters was only the beginning of a siege of harassment. The sit-ins went on, but everyone agreed that Johnnie was not to be in on them for a couple of days.

The rumors about the forthcoming trial multiplied, grew and acquired a mythological depth of their own. They were all going to be subpoenaed, the story went, and every detail of their lives was going to be up for perusal. There was reason too to think that their phones were being tapped. Every time Connie picked up the phone, she could hear either a clicking like Morse code, a hollow sound like a wind tunnel or both. And there were times when the phone wouldn't function at all. As soon as she heard about the trial, the first batch of rumors, she called Jason. He was at home alone.

"There've been some developments," she said.

"On the public scene?"

"Yes."

"Well?"

"I'd rather not talk about them on the phone." She also wanted to see him. They hadn't had any time together by themselves since she'd gotten back from Berkeley.

"Well, come over here then. I'm fixin' my car."

"Okay." She slid the receiver of her beloved telephone back into its cradle, went out and hopped into the car.

When she arrived at his house, she could see his feet sticking out from the front seat; his head was somewhere under the steering wheel. She got into the back seat.

"Hello, you wild radical." He sat up.

"Hi."

"I've missed you, honey."

"I've missed you," feeling him look at her, the first man looking at the first woman.

"Now what are these developments you spoke of?"

She told him about the rumors. "What if we should be called up and asked about, well, about each other, for instance, what would we say?" Fear was a deep thing striking its beats into the blood with the regularity of a pulse.

"Well, we certainly wouldn't tell them the truth."

"No," doubt in her voice.

"You weren't thinking of telling them the truth, were you?"

"Well, not telling them the truth is perjury."

"And telling them the truth is suicide. Child, I sometimes despair of you."

"I wouldn't have told them the truth."

"I hope not." He got up off the seat. "We got plenty of trouble now, honey, just you watch it. We're going to have to keep a tight lid on everything."

"On us?"

"Especially on us."

"Us *is* everything."

He smiled. "Let's go in the house."

They went up the steps and across the gray, weathered porch. Inside his house. In his arms, with his daughter's picture on the wall.

"Oh, baby, I've missed you," kissing her slowly, she having the sense of being at last in his house, in the house she'd driven by so many times, aching because she saw his shirts hung on a clothesline where she hadn't hung them. "I like having you in my house."

There was a brick fireplace, a long, low couch, a chair, a table and the TV; that was the living room. There was a door to the small dining room, and one to . . .

"The bedroom." His eyes followed her gaze.

"Oh."

"Would you like to go in?"

She glanced at him to see if he was serious.

"I'd like to take you here." He said it so softly that she barely heard it, and then he sighed. They were standing there a foot apart, and the pain she felt in her eyes was him looking at her and wanting her that way, and the pain she felt in her heart was his heart cut open. "But . . ." He looked at her and didn't finish the sentence. "You know, the words are beginning to disappear between us," he said. •

She smiled. "I'm learning." Then she felt the desire invade

her and become her skin, the layers of nerve and muscle, the bones themselves, and she felt it take her over, and she went to him. The tension ran high and then disappeared for a moment as he kissed her, and the tension was the knife blade hanging over them. Desire but don't possess, possess but only fleetingly.

"You'd better go," he said.

"I have to go to the bathroom."

He gestured toward the back of the house, and she went through the small dining room into the kitchen, where the paint was peeling from the walls and dishes were stacked on the drainboard of the sink. She pulled the image inside her—it was a small, old, cracked and broken kitchen but the room in all the world where she would most have liked to do her cooking.

When she came back into the living room, he was sitting in the easy chair reading.

"Thank you for the use of your bathroom," she said.

"Anytime at all," looking casually up from his book at her, amused. Then . . . mixed feelings, almost no feeling allowed to flow into its natural channel, each feeling meeting another that cut it off abruptly. Their one pure emotion, love, lay like a vast meadow of tall grass under the changing winds.

A few hours later, after she'd gone to the grocery store and arrived home, Alice called and asked her if she'd collect some coffee money before the sit-in that night. There were levels of involvement: some of those who wouldn't sit in would give money, some would write letters to the newspaper, some would deal with the power structure. Connie was a rabble-rouser, and Reverend Williams was a politician and not nonviolent anyway. She could envision him with his small, efficient gun killing the people she faced nonviolently across that counter every night. Surprisingly, his name was on the list of those who were willing to give money. She had to repress the impulse to tell Alice that he didn't have any money. She was not supposed to know things like that.

She hung up the phone. There were four names on the list; she had said to Alice that she'd see that it got done, but, of course, she wanted to go to his house herself. Her desire even to be in the same room with him was so intense that she grabbed each opportunity as if it had been handed to her in some magical way, fate masquerading as Alice. He was more judicious; he was religious, she was not; but she was the superstitious one, and because of her ability to convince herself that every imagined opportunity to catch a glimpse of him was fated, she took risks he didn't approve of, drove unnecessary distances and showed up at places where she had no good reason to be.

She called him at the church office, hoping he'd be there, hoping he'd say she could come.

"Sure," he said when she reached him, "you can come over and get the money. Matter of fact, it'd be good for you to come when my wife is there; the neighbors probably noticed you there today."

"Yes." She'd known his wife would be there and wanted to see them together in that atmosphere. But he thought of tactics when she wished he wouldn't.

"What time you want to come?"

"About seven-thirty. The sit-in's supposed to start at eight."

"Okay, darlin', I'll see you then. I gotta work on a sermon now."

"Bye, bye."

"Bye, darlin'." The tones of his voice were like so many piano chords, and now, even with the incredible luck of seeing him twice in one day, she was disturbed by having struck that chord which indicated that he felt the need to detach himself from her. . . .

The first three names on the list were those of middle-class black families who lived in the nice neighborhood. She went to their houses first and sat a brief time at each house, wanting to have time to spend at his, and half listened to the people who gave her money as they disavowed their full support of the sit-ins and hoped aloud that their names wouldn't have to be connected with them. She assured them of their safety, feeling as she looked into their faces like a doctor granting them immunity from some dread disease.

And so it was with more than one kind of relief that she found herself out of their houses and driving down the dark, cool road again, this time toward his house, and she pulled up, for the first time in darkness. She knocked at the door, feeling she knocked too hard, and he opened it, standing there now in slacks, a white open-necked shirt and a tweed jacket.

"Hey there, Mrs. Wilder, come on in, it's cold out there," the professional greeting of the preacher. Well, what had she expected?

"Thank you very much," she said stiffly, and entered what was a warm flood of light compared to the cloistered gray living room of the afternoon, for now there was a fire, orange and golden, surging in the open fireplace.

"Sit down," Mrs. Williams said, and she sat in a rocker in front of the fireplace; the rocker had been in the dining room that afternoon. Mrs. Williams sat in the easy chair.

"So you came to take money down to the rabble-rousers," Reverend Williams said. "Should we give it to her?" glancing at his wife. He was standing in front of the fire, facing them, between them, and the firelight picked up the colors of his face so that it was dark, mahogany and chestnut by turns. He stood like some Indian chief in front of his tribal fire, and his eyes burned, desire and mastery. Connie wondered how his wife could not know, but his communication had been with his wife, and the three of them were locked into their triangle as surely as if its sides had been made of steel.

"Oh, we'll give her the money." Mrs. Williams laughed. "Rev is such a tease. You mustn't mind him."

Connie looked up at him. Something in the depths of his eyes warned her that she wasn't being careful enough. "Well, I know"—she turned to Mrs. Williams—"that he doesn't approve of some of the things we do." We, the young, the radical, mythical; she did almost nothing without his approval.

"He don't disapprove near as much as I do," Mrs. Williams said laughing.

She was a nice woman, Connie thought, but when she spoke of disapproval, her face hardened into lines that by now must be habitual—Connie thought of their discussion about marriage at the church dinner. "Well, I think this is going to work," she said. "I think this is worth doing."

"Oh, it'll work," Jason said. "It'll stir up a lot of trouble."

She knew that wasn't what he felt, so why was he lying? She thought back. He supported them; he'd said things in public about the situation that were maybe even stronger than what he felt, for he saw things in the round, and he saw history where she saw only single events in which she could become passionately involved. His wife softened subtly back into her chair when he spoke his agreement. By a series of rhetorical turns, whatever relationship existed between them was kept in balance.

"We can't just have black people being beat up every time they go in to have a cup of coffee, can we?"

"No," he said, "we can't have that."

She knew what he would have done about it if it had been him and anyone had pushed him.

"If people would just turn to God, trust in Jesus," Mrs. Williams said. She sat with her hands folded in her lap, her gray hair drawn back into a sober bun, and her round face contemplative.

Connie felt a sigh rise within her, tones she couldn't respond to, a feeling she felt Jason share across the space between them. "I'd better be going," she said. "Those people'll raise sand if I don't get down there."

"Lookit how she talks," Jason said, again to his wife. "Those people are tryin' to turn her into a Southern black girl. Here's some money, Mrs. Wilder. Don't let them buy nothing but coffee. I ain't giving you money to be wasted." And he went over to the door to let her out.

"So long, Mrs. Wilder."

"So long, Mrs. Williams."

"I won't go out to the car with you. It's too cold."

"Okay, so long." She laughed, for his wife's benefit.

Outside a rush of cold air washed over her body, and as she walked to the car, the ache began inside her that was part of leaving him at any time under any circumstances. She thought about Mrs. Williams, a woman who was twenty-five years older than she was, who was poor and black in a society that distributed its privileges among the rich and white. That woman was the only person in the world whom she envied, the only person in the world whom she would have liked to be.

CHAPTER 28

When she got back to the Winters', they were all waiting for her so they could start. . . . Along the dark, empty streets, under the ominous masses of trees, Connie walked between Johnnie and Ellie to the main, lighted thoroughfare where the Pancake Shack was located. Across the street was The Bar, where Sally Krause had discovered an "Orangedale scene." They usually organized there before they went over to the Shack.

"Gotta have a beer," Johnnie said as they started into The Bar.

"No money," Ellie said shortly. "The money'll barely buy us the coffee."

"Some chick'll buy me beer." He went over to the bar to woo the barmaid, and returned to the booth with a tall can of beer and three glasses. "When she found out I had chicks with me, it blew her interest."

"Connie and Willie Jones are going to be captains tonight," Ellie said to Johnnie. "You and Connie sit toward the back. The windows run along almost to the back, but you try to stay out of range. Let Connie sit in front of the window if either one of you has to."

"Thanks a lot," Connie said, though she had planned it that way herself.

"We don't want Connie's pretty head blown off," Johnnie said. "They just bluffin' though." Both Johnnie and the Winters had received messages by phone and mail that if Johnnie went back into the Pancake Shack he would be killed.

"Let's hope so," Ellie said.

They left The Bar and started across the street. Somehow the process of crossing the street during these evenings became a ritual, a preface to the danger that might lie ahead. Before they crossed, they noted those who watched them, cops in patrol cars all along the block and the single well-known unmarked car of the FBI men, who behaved like nothing so much as young actors ineptly portraying what they in fact were. They crossed the street, now casual, and the watchers watched. They walked along the street and into the Pancake Shack, where ill-assorted white men sat at intervals along the counter and a waitress with a fat round face and greasy hair leaned against a cutting board behind the counter. There was a man who worked there who made Connie shudder whenever she saw him; he appeared regularly at the picket lines, standing by and watching, and he was at the bus station almost every time they were there having coffee. Bald, thin, his teeth broken and splayed in different directions, his chest caved in and his eyes bleary and watery blue. His hands were thin but looked capable of strangling someone. He came out of the back room now; Connie felt him stare at her, hatred and interest in his eyes; for her, he was the enemy.

The place smelled. It always struck them as they entered it. A counter ran the length of it, and between the stools and the back wall, there was barely enough room for a line of men to stand with their backs against the windows that ran all the way along the wall opposite the counter. Johnnie and Connie entered first and walked to the back, taking the stools closest to the jukebox. Beyond the jukebox, around a corner at the back, were the bathrooms and then the room where the Ku Klux Klansmen met informally and arranged recruitment drives. There was a broken, swinging screen door that led from the outside almost directly into that room. That was a door the sit-in people never went through.

"Shit," Johnnie had said, "we don't want to go in there through no back door. That what the fight all about anyway."

Getting to the bathrooms also posed its problems, and for anyone who was sitting toward the front and wanted to hear some music, it was a long walk to the back. No one ever knew what would provoke the rednecks to violence.

The waitress stood, still, against the cutting board, her arms crossed.

"Hey, we'd like some service here," one of the younger, more belligerent students. Everyone sat quietly talking, laughing with each other, "their" crowd against the other. The rednecks snickered.

"Yeah, lady," a hand slapped the table.

The waitress moved nervously, her hand to her hair. "What'll you have?"

"Coffee, jes coffee."

"An' don' poison it, lady."

Cups of coffee came, slowly. One by one, they were served. Two rangy white men came in, and the waitress smiled suddenly, flirted, and Johnnie said: "Lookit her parading her ass."

Connie laughed. Next to Johnnie were two rednecks, and she could feel the pressure of their bodies upon her. On the jukebox they were playing "Charlie Comin' Home with His Mule," hillbilly music that whanged and whined. "Hang On, Sloopy" was the official song of the sit-in, and any of them who made the long walk to the jukebox played it.

The chef emerged from the back room; Connie watched him as he walked toward the waitress. His shoulders curved around the hollow of his chest, his chef's hat flopped loosely on his thinning, dry yellowish hair, and his ears were weird appendages growing like vegetables out of the sides of his head. He murmured to the waitress. She laughed the high whining laugh of the hillbillies. There was a rumble of sound from the back room; a group of men came out, three of them big, bulky, beefy, with their red necks and pouches of skin hanging from their chins; they stood two feet from Connie. A small man broke from them, like a stalk breaking from a bunch of celery. He ran behind the counter. He held a knife, the blade pointed upward, his hand closed tightly around the knife's thick handle. He gestured with the knife as he spoke:

"Ah'm from Alahbama, an' in Alahbama, we don' have none of this shit. All you niggers and nigger lovers comin' here . . . Ah don' know how sum feel, but ah ain' gonna stan' for it. Now any y'all wanna come in, you gonna face this here knife." His voice was rough and coarse. He came out from behind the counter, and one of the big men gave him a sign. "Now you see this here sign. It sez enter at yer own risk."

"Hey, man, the cat can read."

"Ain't that wonderful?"

"Awright now, y'all jes shut up. I'd like to stick mah knife raght into someone's back." He was walking past Connie now; she imagined the knife slipping into her back. After he had passed, her legs started trembling uncontrollably under the counter.

Later, she was walking back with one of the students from the police station, where they'd been to testify against one of the rednecks. The man with the knife had been arrested when he'd gone out onto the street waving it; he had, however, been immediately released while Connie and her friend were down at the station testifying against another man who had cursed mildly. They had been asked to testify against him, but no one had given evidence in the case of the man with the knife. The cops, momentarily and arbitrarily on their side for a change, were picking up rednecks to be let out in an hour and selecting those whom they wished to press charges against later. Political pressure from one side and another controlling it all. For Connie, it was another revelation. When the cops were against you, at least you knew where they were and that it was your job to avoid them at any cost. But in your bones, you felt confident that, although they were ignorant and bigoted, at least they dealt with their own group in terms of some kind of reason. Now she was no longer sure of that either. It looked as if they dealt with everyone according to the caprices of those in power. They would eventually circle back and mow down their usual fields, her people laid out like so much hay. In the meantime, their machine moved irresponsibly across other fields, surprising whatever lay in its path.

"Look at that," the girl with her said. They were across from the Pancake Shack now, and they could see people all along the counter, sitting on the stools with their coffee in front of them, and behind them, like a line of sentries with their backs against the wall, the rednecks, big and small, burly and ugly, with their red necks and fat, phlegmatic faces.

"Let's go," Connie said.

"What if there aren't any seats?"

"We'll go over to the cigarette machine, and we'll work from there."

As they came in, a lot of people looked up. A boy with dark curly hair at the counter smiled cheerfully and waved at them. Ellie was still at the counter, but Johnnie had gone. It was now eleven-thirty. Thank God he was gone, Connie thought; the line of sentries would have provoked him to violence, their non-violence lying like a fragile layer of new skin over their wounds.

"There's a seat," Jean said.

"Okay, you take it." She pulled the plunger out on the cigarette machine and watched the pack drop down into the slot below.

"Connie," the boy with the curly hair called, "Ray wants to speak to you."

She nodded and started back. Ray was young and tall and strong and good-looking and black, and as she walked between the two lines of people, one seated with their backs to her and the other watching her, she felt hatred radiate from the cold faces of the sentries.

"How you doin'?"

"Okay. I'll tell you what happened later. Really funny things are going on." With all the tremors inside her, she knew she appeared calm and amused, their stance.

"I gotta take my wife to work," Ray said. "You want my seat?"

"Yeah, as soon as I put on some music." The hillbilly thing was getting to her. She walked to the back and put her quarter in. The hillbilly number ended, and she watched the record as it was lifted up and put down onto the turntable: "Hang on, Sloopy..."

She walked back, and as Ray slid off the seat, she slid onto it with the sense of impending danger that had begun now to be almost a settled part of her life. The slatternly waitress came, and she ordered coffee and opened John Donne, and she thought of Jason and almost forgot in the intensity of memory and the poem where she was.

CHAPTER 29

The sit-ins ended, and a number of their demands were met, and a couple of the waitresses at the Pancake Shack were fired, but the rednecks had been released almost as soon as they were arrested, and the Winters' and Johnnie's trials were still pending.

It had been six weeks since she and Jason had been together. He was to meet her at Vanessa's. She sat at the kitchen table.

"Calm down," Vanessa said to her now, although Connie hadn't said a word.

"Oh, Lord." Connie got up and paced the kitchen. "Six weeks."

Vanessa shook her head and smiled. The buzzer sounded downstairs. Connie raced to the upstairs door, then down the stairs without turning on the light. When she opened the door, he was standing there so close that she could have brushed her mouth across his.

"Hi," he said. "We're not going tonight."

She could feel her emotions collide and fall through her body like heavy water. "No," she said, "oh, please." And then, with an attempt at control: "Why not?"

"I think someone's been following me. Sixth sense. I simply wouldn't trust going there tonight."

Her impulse was to cry, but she knew that it wouldn't do any good. Deep within her, at the bottom of that well where all emotion started, she knew that he was probably right, his rightness part of his knowledge of a set of rules that she was ignorant of. "Please..." but it trailed off.

"No, that's just it. Bye, baby, I'll call you in the morning." And he was gone.

She stood slumped against the wall, the tears running down her face. With his trench coat on and his hat pulled down over his eyes, he had looked like a spy, wary and deliberate, the performance suiting the mood; the world they were living in demanded spying ability. In this world, she was an innocent.

She went slowly back up the stairs, the tears still coming. Vanessa was one of the few people she wasn't ashamed to cry in front of.

"What happened?" Vanessa was standing in the lighted doorway.

"We're not going."

"Why not?"

"Someone was following him. He said his sixth sense told him."

Vanessa sighed. "He was probably right. You know that."

Connie nodded, but it only made her cry more.

"Come upstairs and talk to me while I iron."

They went up the stairs. Vanessa began ironing, the clothes piled around her in chairs, and Connie sat cross-legged on the floor next to the space heater, with her coat still on, and wept.

"It'll take you a long time to get used to it." Vanessa spoke softly, her voice soothing, as she pressed the iron hard against the cloth.

"To what?"

"To living this way, and there's one part of you that never gets used to it. I know, I've lived it."

"It's different for you because you're not white."

"I know." Vanessa stopped ironing and looked at her. "It's harder for you and him than for any two blacks or any two whites, and I don't have any advice for you about that. You'll just have to learn how to do it yourself."

"Okay." Connie got up. "I feel better now. You always make me feel better. I'll go home and let my baby-sitter go home. Thanks, Vanessa."

"Anytime. I only wish I could cut down on your suffering."

"You do. Just by being here," and she ran down the stairs, building up energy, strength, so that she could get through the next few days . . . until they had a new plan, until she found herself in his arms, with his mouth on hers, so that she could have peace.

She sat in the square, lighted bedroom on Robin's bed, reading a story to Willie and Robin, reading a story about a child who lived in an enclosed white middle-class world, a child who lived from toy to toy: " '. . . And Joey's mother said: "You'll have to clean up your room, Joey. It's a complete mess." ' "

"Couldn't we have another story?" Connie asked them. The baby-sitter from two doors down was due. She was supposed to meet Jason at nine-thirty, torn between her obligations here and the obligations of her heart, torn really between heart and heart.

"My fish book, my fish book." Willie jumped up and ran to the bookshelf, where the books all leaned precariously to one side. He grabbed the fish book, and the rest of the books spun out across the floor.

"Oh, Willie," irritation compounded by nervousness. "Why'd you have to do that?"

Chagrined, he started to pick them up.

"No, let's read," Connie said. "When Alma comes, she can help you."

Willie happily climbed up beside her and handed her the book. She began on the page he selected: " 'The shark is a large fish; it has long rows of dangerous teeth. When the shark is in the water near swimmers, it can indeed be very dangerous. It can tear a man to pieces in a few minutes.' "

"Can it really, Mama?" Robin looking up at her.

"Yes, baby, it really can," with a sense of reassuring her. Yes, baby, a shark can really tear a man up, but a shark was a natural force, and you could contrive to avoid it. Joey and Joey's nice white middle-class mother could also tear up a man or a town or a tribe of men or a race, but there was no teaching that now; simpler to replace Joey with a bunch of moderately safe sharks.

And finally, five fish descriptions later, she kissed them good night while Alma picked up the books. Outside, on her way to her car, the memory of her own bedtime stories . . .

She sat on her pink bedspread in flannel pajamas with clowns on them and rubber-soled feet at their bottoms, and her mother sat with her and read her stories about little girls who her mother thought were like her, but she grew restless and asked for fairy tales or adventure stories, and her brother fussed at her whatever she did, and from the time she was three, she felt somehow that he belonged more to the house and to the family than she did. He seemed to be the right size; she was thin and angular. He laughed at the right times; she thought too much;

and as they grew, she looked for ways other than the ones she was taught at home. There must be other ways, there just had to be, and when she discovered Greenwich Village, it was mecca for her, and she became a bohemian the moment she heard there was such a thing. . . .

Storm-tossed trees, a tangle of branches, leaves shaken by wind as his car pulled up. She got in beside him, without a word, praying.

"Hello, baby."

"Hi." She put her hand in his, and the feeling swept through her that nothing within her belonged to her, that she was only an extension of him. They rode down the highway silently and turned off the road to Mrs. Charles'. Turning in: landmarks, trees bent a certain way, grouped as if for camouflage or conversation, dark trees bending over the road, farm buildings set back, dark, weather-beaten, unused at night, forming a thousand frightening, grotesque shapes until you knew them. Then their silent darkness was reassuring.

They locked the outer door and closed the bedroom door enough so that a small slice of light shone through the crevice and into the bedroom. He took her into his arms. Relief melted through her body, melted its substance as her desire mounted.

"It's something to get here," he said.

"Do you ever feel it's not worth it?"

"Never." He kissed her slowly. "Not ever. If I felt it wasn't worth it, then I wouldn't be here."

She laughed. "You're so logical," but his logic, like everything else about him, warmed her.

In bed, moments of touch substituted for hours of language; thoughts bent from the brain into the curve of the body, the breast, the slope of a shoulder and where their love lay, in something beyond the union of flesh. Finding some sort of oneness in ecstasy beyond where time reached, in the curve of a violently colored eternity. A sudden knocking and rattling at the outer door, and he was up and absolutely alert before she had registered the sound as real. He stood at the door, naked, with the gun in his hand.

"Yes?" his voice wary and cool yet under strain, the voice of some absolutely disciplined stranger.

"Is someone in they-uh?" the low coarse ugly voice of a white Southerner.

"Yes, I'm a friend of Mrs. Charles', just takin' a nap." The outside door had been wrenched free; somehow he'd torn the hook and the eye from the wood. She heard the click of the gun as Jason cocked it. . . . "If we ever get caught," he'd said, "and they try anything, I'm taking ten of them down before I go."

Then, in the distance, she heard Mrs. Charles' voice: "Jes' a fren' of mine, sleepin'. Come on up here, I got your shirts ready for you, all ironed up nice."

They heard him mounting the stairs, slowly, heavily, and then a very distant conversation. She sighed, and the sigh shook her body. He came over and sat on the edge of the bed, the gun still in his hand, but hanging there now as his hand relaxed. She put her arms around him, her face against his shoulder. His body was damp but cooled by fear.

"How long have we been here?" she asked.

He looked at his watch. "Twenty minutes. Get dressed."

"Do we have to go?"

"Of course we have to go."

"But he's gone. Mrs. Charles has taken care of him."

"He's gone for the moment, honey. That's all we know. He knows someone's here. He may go and get ten or fifteen other men. What would we do then?"

A tremor went through her body. It was an idea that wouldn't have occurred to her, an idea that might not turn out to be the correct prediction but was based on facts, an entire history of brutal and horrible and inhuman facts about what people of her color did to people of his color and about what most people felt about their love. She got up and began dressing.

"Why don't you come to my house?" she said. "I'll send the baby-sitter home as soon as I get there, and you could come over."

"What about the kids?"

"They're asleep."

"I don't know."

She watched him tying his shoe. "Do you want to come?"

He looked at her. "You know I do. I'll try. After I drop you at your car, I'll go to the bus station and call you from there."

She nodded, slung her purse over her shoulder, and they went out.

They drove, and she could feel the tension as an almost unbearable force, and she dug her fingernails into the palms of her hands and couldn't feel them. He drove, cool and composed.

"I'll call you in twenty minutes," he said when he let her out.

"Okay." Her tangle of feelings knotted and reknotted while she drove home, and the least of her feelings was fear.

Alma: "Oh, hello, Mrs. Wilder. Meeting got out early, huh?"

"Yes, Alma," and why was it she felt there was a note of doubt in Alma's voice.

It seemed as if Alma had been gone for a year or two when the phone rang. "Hi, baby."

"Darling, I need you. Please come."

"I don't think I can," the words admitting the possibility of his coming, but the tone excluding it.

She listened to the words. "Why not?" the beginnings of panic.

"It's not a good setup. How could I get in there? What would it look like my coming at this hour? People must know your husband's away."

"No, they don't. They don't pay any attention."

"That's where you're wrong. People around here are always paying attention to other people's business. You're not used to small towns. And even if they never paid attention before, when a black man comes to visit a white woman at night and her husband's not at home, they're gonna pay attention they ain't never heard of before."

She knew he was right, but she couldn't let it go. She tried another tack: "It's been so long, and I need you so."

"And you think I don't feel it? You think I don't need you?"

"No, I know you feel it." Her deepest instincts told her he did, but her desire to make him do what she wanted him to fought still. "But sometimes it doesn't seem like you do anything about feeling it," putting her hand up to her ear and closing it over the gold flower that bloomed there, his earring. It wasn't gifts that mattered but feelings. He'd given her more of those than any one woman was entitled to.

"I'll try and come. That's the most I can say."

"If you don't come, call me in the morning, okay?"

"Yes, baby," with the slightest of sighs, "and, Connie, take it easy. You've got to grow up."

"I am grown up." She felt like kicking the wall in. He and Alan said the same things sometimes. Take it easy, take it easy. But how could you!

"Okay, bye."

"Bye, please come," but he'd already hung up.

She made herself a pot of coffee, preparing herself for the vigil. She poured it out, lighted a cigarette and walked up and down, around the dining room fifty times—she counted those —he's *not* coming, she told herself. But the outside chance was what she was hanging on to, the outside chance.

Eleven-thirty, unlikely now that he'd come. She turned out the living-room lights and went and stood at the front door, with the curtain that was puckered across the top of it slightly pulled back, and she stared at the dark road outside, a single street lamp down the street seeming to bloom out of the Spanish moss behind it. Occasionally a car would come down the street.

At twelve, she suddenly thought of the back door and rushed to open it. The dark cool air swirled around her, and she could see the dark shape of the grape arbor in the backyard. He might be coming there. Finally, she took her pillow and curled up on the couch, leaving the dining-room light burning, her mind wondering what she was doing, why she should possibly think he would come out in the middle of the night.

When she awoke, the sun was burning a hole in the eastern part of the sky, and the sky was opening up into ribbons, and her sensations told her that she must have awakened from a dream, that he might never have existed at all.

CHAPTER 30

During spring vacation, they went to New York, having delayed seeing her parents for too long that year. In New York, they got off the plane at night. The noise of the planes and the announcements and the people almost deafened her. The speed with which people moved confused her, and the power of the bright lights hurt her eyes. Her father was there to meet them, and she looked at him as he waved and thought how she liked him—he looked tiny in his big, expensive hat with a small green feather in it, and his face was cherubic. She loved him, in fact, until he started talking about money and "doing well."

On the drive into the city, she sat in the back seat looking out while her father and Alan talked in the front seat and the children interrupted with Grandpa this and Grandpa that; drinking in her city with her vision altered by time. She looked out at the highways and then at the monster of a city, huge and bleak and cold. They were driving up Central Park West toward her parents' apartment house, by the long thick brown stone wall that protected the park from the people.

"The city's so dangerous now," her father was saying, "I can't let your mother go out after dark," and then, "Connie, I said I can't let your mother go out at all after dark."

"Mm," she responded.

"My, young lady, you certainly are quiet there in the back seat." After thirty-two years, she was still "young lady" to him.

"I'm tired, Daddy." She was sitting thinking about the last time she and Jason had been together, brief, intense, maybe the last time ever at Mrs. Charles'—Jason said it was too dangerous there now.

"You didn't eat dinner on the plane, did you?" her father asked.

"No, Mom said not to." Always when she was at home, she felt her behavior being obscurely monitored.

"Yes, your mother has prepared a good dinner for you." He drove the car into the underground garage, and they rode up in an elevator that transported her into her past.

Her mother was at the door. The children jumped and

clung to her, her mother kissed Alan. Words from the past: he's like another son to me. She kissed her mother.

"Hello, Mom."

"You look thin."

She nodded. Her mother was plump, not at all in the style of New York women; Connie *felt* thin, angular, lank, intellectual and hostile. They were walking into this supercomfortable wall-to-wall-carpeted apartment that she knew so well, and she felt like a disease in the family, carrying bags to the two extra bedrooms, where they would sleep, straightening things out for the children, helping them wash their hands.

In the living room, cocktails before dinner, she and Alan on a sofa, her mother and father on chairs, and off in a side room her children watching cartoons and laughing, she felt them as a photograph in a magazine, entrenched in patterns. Her mother had always hoped that she would live exactly as she herself had lived, a husband who made money, two children, a lovely home and not too many demands made on the world. . . . Now she dimly heard her father describing to Alan a new kind of curtain fiber that his company had begun manufacturing, her mother smiling, nodding, approving; her mother apparently approved of the curtain fiber.

They were sitting around the dinner table eating her mother's good dinner: roast beef, mashed potatoes, salad, broccoli and hot rolls with butter, the heart of America's goodness. . . .

She watched her mother and father, and thought how she had rebelled against them sometimes and then swung back to please them, and Alan pleased them; she could watch him pleasing them now.

"Yes," he was saying, "you miss the advantages of a big city in Orangedale, but you don't have to worry when you go downtown at night. It's peaceful, and the weather is nice almost all year round. It definitely has its advantages." He wasn't talking about the Orangedale she knew; he sounded like a brochure from the chamber of commerce. She felt lost and angry; all three of the other adults at this table had bought things, patterns of ideas she couldn't buy; she could look at her mother and father now and see versions of what she and Alan would become if they went on in the way they were going now, and she suddenly realized that she would have to leave Alan no matter what her relationship with Jason promised or didn't promise. Her head reeled, and she felt sick for a moment. Then she felt relief as she looked around the table at the faces. She loved them all, and she was going to put them through all kinds of pain, but the pull of her own unlived life, the claims it laid upon that soul within her, which was only now really growing, were too much.

"Connie's brother and Carole just love Cleveland," her mother was saying.

"I've never been to Cleveland," Alan said.

"Well, you'll have to go," her mother went on. "You'll have to go and visit Raymond and Carole." Her brother Raymond, four years older, a successful doctor now, in Cleveland, Ohio. She scarcely knew him, and she didn't think she liked him.

She seemed to be the only one of these four Bartletts whose drive was to know what was, what was out there, what was the truth, if indeed any could be found. Her mother had listened to her talk about civil rights on the phone, but her response was that there must be another way, and she didn't see why Connie had to be involved.

"How's Raymond's practice going?" Connie asked her mother.

"Fine, fine. Carole writes that he has so many patients he hardly gets a chance to take a vacation."

"That's good," she said, "that's really good," and felt it was. She helped herself to more broccoli with a sudden hunger. Now that the decision was made, it seemed as if everything would get easier.

CHAPTER 31

Orangedale, the warmth of the new weather after the brief cold of winter. Her dance class was preparing for a performance, and "Reach Out for Me" was on the record player. Diana Alexander was dancing to it, halfway there, with half a dance that threatened to become monotonous, dancing to the music with the red and blue lights playing on her while Connie sat cross-legged on the stone floor watching and the girls sat around her on the floor or ranged along the wall on folding chairs.

"I ain't doing no solo." Diana sat down.

"Yes, you are," one of the things Connie found herself saying over and over again. "Rest a little, and then you can try it again, or else I'll help you Saturday."

"I'll do mine," Lucinda Williams, distantly related to Reverend Jason Williams, lithe and gentle and beautiful, a young girl's body and something of Jason's face, with the Indian bone structure and an almost supernal grace. Next to LaVern, she had the most promise. She squatted on her heels and put her record on. The music reached up and closed in over the room, Lucinda danced with a gentle control and an intensity in her turns that laid an ache into Connie's soul, and when she was finished, curled up on the floor with her hands out in front of her, there was a hush in the room and only the sound of the needle grinding back and forth on the end of the record, and then the girls clapping suddenly and spontaneously.

"That's beautiful," Connie said, and Diana stood up.

"I ain't doing no solo in the show," she said. "Not after that."

Connie sighed. "We'll work on it Saturday until you feel good about it. I better do mine once; it's almost nine."

"Oh do yours." "I want to see Connie's." "Do it now, Connie," and she went to put her record on, smiling, feeling warmth at their confidence—always pleased at their confidence yet not wanting to misrepresent herself; she was not a trained dancer, and she had told them that, but they insisted on their vision.

The music began . . . that eternal beat in the blood raised

to the surface; "When a Man Loves a Woman," and her leg went up in an extension, up through time and into pure space where there was nothing but the poise of the air, and she felt the red and blue lights fall across her body as she danced, giving her the illusion that she was actually on stage, and she was half aware of the girls watching her dance, and then she lost even that awareness as she and the dance became one, and she was on the floor, on her knees, and all their agony was in her dance, and then she was up again, and the moment of substance was air, and the moment of air was substance, and the leaps came, and she felt herself flying through each leap, catapulting through pure space, meeting each climax, there were five at the end, five leaps, five rises into the air of sound, and then she melted into the floor, suddenly recovering her senses, and could hardly get up, and the girls clapped and clapped, and as she got up, her legs still trembling from the dance, she felt a kind of soft sensation of well-being flood into her. . . .

"It's nine," she said. "We'll work some more on Saturday. Diana, you can come and work at my house in between if you want to."

Diana nodded, and the girls scattered around the room like some flock of birds and pulled their slacks on over their tights and slipped into their shoes while she rushed to get her things together so she could get to a meeting where he was.

In the bathroom, hot and sweaty, stripping off her leotard and tights and pulling her clothes on, brushing her soaking hair, washing, spraying on cologne, washing her dirty feet and slipping them into sandals, breathless, with a pain in her chest because she was rushing and still exhausted from the dance, then driving the girls home, roaring around corners and gulping down cherry soda. At last, the children were all at home, and finally she arrived at the church where he was, and saw him and felt her heart open as she sat down, as if the air surrounding him formed some absolute cushion of comfort. To be where he was.

Mrs. Charles' place was now out of the question. No more

lovely bedroom with a slice of light in the doorway. One thanked God for favors, large or small, too late. If they'd chafed at the restrictions the place put on them, those of silence and darkness, they were now left with a vacant aching space and no immediate plan to put something else in its stead. And now, of all times, when she needed to be talking to him about leaving Alan. In New York, she'd been sure. In Orangedale, in the middle of already-lived scenes, it was more difficult. She *thought* she was going to leave Alan.

Jason called her nearly every day, and the phone was almost like a person to her. She arranged her tasks in the house so that she was never far from it when she thought there was any chance of his calling. She let Willie take out the garbage, and she waited to hang the clothes out until after he'd called. She made lists of things she had to tell him, and she breathed her love into the mouthpiece. The phone rang, and all her nerves jumped an inch. It might be a wrong number or Alice Rivers wanting her to do some work or another student wanting an assignment or to chat about a paper. If it was Vanessa, she could tell her she was waiting and call her back, but if it was any of the others, it was a fight to get them off. She was standing there thinking about it, with her hand on the receiver, when the phone rang. She picked up the receiver.

"Hello."

"Hey, baby, what're you doing?"

"Nothing. Waiting for you to call."

He laughed. "You spend a lot of time waiting, don't you?"

"Yes."

"And is it worth it?"

"If it wasn't worth it, I guess I wouldn't do it, would I?"

"I guess you wouldn't. I love you, darlin', I really love you."

"I know. I love you." There was a pause, and what passed between them shook her even though it made no sense that there should be anything passing between them over the phone. "Jason, what if I was to leave Alan?" one of those times when the whole world must be in silence.

"I don't know." He sighed. "I honestly don't know. Are you asking me for some kind of promise that you know I can't make?"

"No"—the tears were running down her face—"I'm not asking you for anything. I'm just asking you for your opinion."

"Baby, you crying?" The sound of her sobs told him. "I can't talk to you when you cry, honey. You want to talk later?"

"No, I—I want to talk now," and she forced herself to stop.

"It's too big for the phone. Let's go to T. C.'s and talk tomorrow."

"Okay."

"But I can't make your decisions for you, because I have nothing to promise you."

"I know."

"Can you come to T. C.'s tomorrow afternoon?"

"Yes."

"All right, baby, we'll talk then. Bye."

She hung up.

Diana Alexander came that afternoon, and they decided to have an impromptu rehearsal, and she went and picked up the girls who could come, and they worked in the living room. . . . Her dance class, moments of ecstasy and periods of pushing and yelling and feeling the children resisting work as if their souls would be sucked out of their bodies by it and then seeing one of them or a group rise in the air or swing suddenly to the floor with so much energy and such perfect timing that they seemed framed by eternity.

She realized at the end of the afternoon, after she'd taken them home and was back cleaning up the living room, that she'd barely thought of him during the rehearsal, that she'd barely thought of Alan or the snarled mess that was becoming her life.

CHAPTER 32

She drove the tunnel to T. C.'s feeling . . . what? Her feelings changed faster than her mind could fathom, and her fate! While her fate had once been so clearly decided, now it had been wrenched free, and clung to the world by a single thread of flesh.

She turned the final corner, and T. C.'s dogs came yelping and racing out around the car. T. C. was sitting on the steps of the shack, and he raised a hand in greeting. Jason was sitting on a log, dressed in a dark suit, smoking, with his hat pushed to the back of his head, and he just looked at her.

"Hi," she said.

"Hey, baby," the soft, the liquid notes, the voice that washed through her soul and enclosed her in a perfect atmosphere.

"C'mon and sit on a chair." T. C. pulled a rusty chair up.

"Where's my soda, honey?"

"I got 'em in a bag in my car." She smiled.

"Well, get them then. I can't wait all day for my soda." T. C. laughed. "You tryin' to get that girl trained, Rev?"

"She's *my* girl. I gotta get her trained."

Connie brought the Cokes back, cold against her hand, with the moisture on them like rain, something to bring feeling to her hand, to mask her deeper feelings.

"She's your girl, aw right, couldn' nobody mistake that." T. C. got up. "I'm goin' to town now. See y'all later." He walked slowly across the strewn yard to his old car and cranked it up and then, with a wave of his big, flat hand and a smile on his eternally uncreased face, he was gone.

"You don't believe I'd leave Alan for you?"

"I've done some things in my life that I'm not proud of, but I've never broken up a family," his eyes burning their sadness right through to the marrow of her bones.

"You haven't answered my question."

"I'm not asking you to leave Alan or to alter your life for me in any significant way."

"But I've already altered my life completely." She felt close to tears.

He looked at her for a long time. "Yes," he said, "I suppose you have, but it would never have occurred to me that it could happen this way. C'mere. . . ."

She went, and he put his arms around her waist and put his head on her breasts, shaking her to her roots. . . .

"You're such a lovely woman, and I love you so."

She felt her tears beginning. They were in such a beautiful place, with the high tree branches arching overhead and no one in the world to bother them.

"Let's go inside. We were just going to talk today. I wasn't going to love you, but I think I better." He took her hand, and they went up the steps of the shack, and he locked the door behind them.

"It's the first time in the daytime," she said.

He was hanging his jacket up on one of T. C.'s hangers and unknotting his tie—his hands were so sure, and his arms were so strong; the strength of his arms gave her a feeling of peace in the pit of her stomach. "Are you glad we're doing it in the daytime?"

"I'm always glad about anything we do together."

He took her in his arms then and kissed her so hard that she felt as if they gave to each other a new life force.

"I want to give you a baby."

"Oh, Connie!"

"Would you like me to?"

"You know I would."

"And if I did . . . ?"

"I'd love that baby like no man ever loved a baby before," and she looked at him and knew that it was true.

. . . This time when he loved her it was different; whatever of ultimate commitment there could be between two human beings was there between them; she felt her feeling rise and fall with her body—outside the sound of birds, first broken, then whole globes of sound, above their breathing the *only* sound, and then silence; whether the birds stopped or not she didn't know, just the rhythm of giving, desire to desire, hand to hand, and the final welding where she didn't believe they weren't one body, and then weeping in his arms at their joy and their despair while he stroked her neck and her hair.

"Listen, I have to tell you something." He took her face in his hands.

"You don't love me enough to marry me, do you?" not sure he really should, not feeling really worthy.

"Darlin', I love you enough to marry you or die for you or kill for you, but you're my personal happiness, an' I have never put my personal happiness first. There's nothin' in this world I'd rather do than spend the rest of my life with you, but I'd lose everything I have here if I did, and all the people would think I'd sold out. So when the next leader came along, they wouldn't trust him. You gotta understand, I'm not just a preacher, darlin'. For some of these people, I'm like a god. You have to see it. Everything I do is important to them, and I'm so controversial because of my political life that I can't stand any controversy in my private life. These people don't like me being involved with civil-rights demonstrators; they want my whole life to be in the church." She was leaning her chin on her hand now, just watching him and listening, and they were lying side by side still, naked and not touching.

"Then you can't stand having me in your life."

"I can't stand *not* having you in my life either. I couldn't stand having a piece of my heart missing; it wouldn't even be good for my preaching."

She sighed, and he kissed her mouth and the hollow of her throat. . . .

"Do you understand any of what I'm saying?"

"Yes. I don't want to understand any of it, but I saw you in church, and I understand some of it, and I know you love me."

"Always remember that, darlin'. Whatever happens, remember that."

"Maybe I'll go away after a while. I could go back to Berkeley, I have friends there—if you don't change your mind."

"Threat?"

"I don't know. Maybe it's an attempt to do something realistic."

"I don't think I'd ever want you to go, but I can't keep you here. Why don't you stay with Alan? It would be better for the kids."

"I can't. I can't see you both; it isn't fair to Alan, and it doesn't seem to be possible for me."

"Why don't you give me up then? It might be better for everybody concerned."

"I can't give you up." She stared hard at him. "I'd be more likely to commit suicide than to give you up, and I think Alan and I are so far apart that it wouldn't be good for the kids. Two people pulling in different directions is never good for kids."

"There are things about the way you make decisions that I guess I can't begin to understand," he said slowly, "any more than you can understand my debt to the church an' my members. So in the end I can't advise you. But I love you whatever you choose to do."

"And I worship you. I understand about those other people because I'm like them. I think you're some kind of god. I feel like one of those women in the Greek legends. One time a god came and made love to them, and after that they were never the same again, and the god was blasted on Mount Olympus for falling in love with a mere mortal."

"Oh, Connie." He laughed. Then he got up from the bed and started dressing. "There's something else I have to tell you."

"What?"

"There're some people who want me to run for county commission."

"And...?"

"Vanessa heard I was going to run and came into the church this morning and hugged me and said she was so happy about it."

"So you're going to do it?"

"I have to." He said it very softly.

"Yes." She sighed. "You have to. It will make it hard on us, won't it?"

"Yes, but I think we could come here sometimes. You ready to go?"

"As ready as I'll ever be."

He unlocked the door, and they stood looking out. It was like a picture of bright, hot green trees and the soft blue of the sky beyond, and the doorway's space framed it. She could smell the old damp wood smell of the shack and the oil on the tools that lay on T. C.'s tool bench. . . .

He walked her to her car and kissed her while the dogs watched.

"Take care," he said.

"I'll try." His hand was on her open car window, and she took it and kissed his palm. "I do that because I'm mortal."

"Don't forget that I'm a mortal too. You of all people must remember that, because with you, I can be entirely myself, and I need that."

"All right," she said, and drove off without looking back at him, down the road that led through the tunnel.

CHAPTER 33

They were all in the bus station having coffee after a meeting when T. C. came in.

"Willie James done killed Revren' Grey," he said. "Shot him right between the eyes, an' he's layin' outside Fontana's house right now. Poh-lice comin', ain't there yet. Coffee," to the waitress.

Jason was up. "I've gotta go see Mrs. Grey," he said. "What a way for him to go."

Connie watched him; he was already composed, already prepared to deal with what had happened. She had asked him once how he could deal with tragedy that way, and he had said that he dealt with it every day and didn't have the energy to get terribly upset about each thing that happened. She felt sick to her stomach.

"Well," T. C. said, "he would be messin' around with that fool sister of mine. Seems like he got about what he could expect." But Jason had gone.

"Fontana's not a fool, T. C.," Connie defending Fontana, defending herself.

"Hnnh, the way she's played around with Grey, she is. That old sapsucker, seventy if he's a day. Bad business."

"What happened?" Vanessa asked.

"Fontana's been goin' with Revren' Grey for a while, but she never did much like him, an' so after a while she was goin' with Willie James too, an' tonight she an' Willie was in the bed, an' Revren' Grey figgers he'll come by an' see her, an' when Revren' Grey got there, Johnnie McClure was standin' there jivin' with some girl an' he says: 'Hey there, man, where you think you goin'?' An' Revren' Grey, he say: 'Goin' in to see your mama, boy, where I got my rights.' An' Johnnie went on: 'Not tonight, ol man, not tonight.' An' then Revren' Grey threatens Johnnie with his gun, so Johnnie jes' let him go ahead in, an' two of Fontana's girls was in the livin' room, an' Willeen, she jump up and holler: 'Mama, Revren' Grey be here,' so Willie he got time to reach over on the bedside table an get his gun, an' ol' Revren' Grey, he hold on to Willeen an' go right into that bedroom, an' then when he got there, he see Fontana sitting up in the bed with the sheets all down to her waist an' Willie with that gun, so he turned Willeen loose and shot at Willie, but he musta been drunk, 'cause that bullet sailed clean past Willie and went right into the wall, an' Willie just shot to kill an' got old Grey right between the eyes, an' he lay down dead, an' then Willie and Johnnie carried him out and laid him in the road 'cause Willie said he didn' want that sapsucker's body in Fontana's house."

They were silent when T. C. finished, and then, finally, Vanessa got up. "Mama's been so sick. I just came out to this meeting because it was such an important one. My sister's there now, but I've got to get right home to her," and to Connie it seemed that Vanessa was more weary than she'd been five minutes before, as if the weight of what happened in the community descended onto her shoulders, as if what went on at Fontana's house affected her fate directly.

Two days later, she and Jason on the phone. Vanessa's mother had died, and he'd been to sit with Vanessa early, and it was the second or third time he'd gone, and Connie'd always missed him there, but he'd spent almost all the rest of his time with Mrs. Grey, and that was where his mind had been *all* the time.

"Connie, she's all broken up. She keeps saying: 'If it had happened any other way, if he'd been shot by a white man, anything but being to that woman's house, the shame of it, he left me shamed. All the people in his churches, waiting, bearing the shame of it, and he ain't even here to tell them what to do.'"

"Yes," Connie said, wanting desperately to point out the differences between their situations, knowing that he saw and dwelt only upon the similarities and received from Mrs. Grey only the counterpart to his own wife's point of view, while she herself sympathized with Fontana, and in their situation played her role. But Fontana was bad news to most of the black community. She knew if she asked Jason about her he'd say "She ain't worth two cents. . . ." "Jason," she said now, "you can't compare . . . ," but he wasn't listening to her.

"Two churches," he was saying, "An' the members are

wandering around like sheep or children, not knowing what to do, it's like their whole foundation's been eaten away, the basis of their lives just torn up in their faces. I know you don't know nothin' about Grey except maybe what Fontana told you, whatever that may be"—("Some days he an old pain")— "but he was a good preacher, a good man, an' he kept his people's values up, but now they figure, well, if he'd do that, carry on with the worst woman in town an' take a gun to her house, what the hell difference does it make what *we* do, we ain't even special, an' he was ordained."

Her whole soul sighed within her.

"I'm not the worst woman in town," she said quietly, finally, trying to find something to hold on to, the handhold as you hung there in the air, but he cut her down:

"You're worse than the worst woman in town, you're white, an' you're doing work here that threatens to change the structure of everyone's life, black and white. If they found out about you and me, their opinion of me would plunge down to nothing in minutes."

"All right." She was close to tears now. "Like I know I'm going to talk to Alan about the divorce right away, and if you should by chance want me to leave with you, we'll take the kids and get out, and if you can't do that, then I think I'll go to California, and I have a friend there who's divorced and we might be able to live at her house and I can get a job, and then you won't have to be bothered with me any more."

He sighed. "Baby, it's not that. You know it's not that. I want you to go off with me. I *want* to take you far away, but I don't see how I can go."

"Then I'll just go with the kids."

"Let's cross that bridge when we come to it, all right?"

"Well, you want me to go, don't you?"

"No, I wouldn't ever *want* you to go. I don't ever want to lose you, not ever. Do you understand that?"

"Yes."

"All right, darlin'. I gotta run. There's Mrs. Franklin's funeral today and Reverend Grey's tomorrow. Will I see you today?"

"Yes."

"All right, darlin'."

"Bye, I love you."

"I love you too." And he hung up. She stood with the phone in her hand still, not wanting to admit, each time, that the temporary, tenuous connection had been broken. . . .

CHAPTER 34

A stretch of sky, late afternoon, the sky opening so that the clouds were lower than the sky, and there were stretches of loose, fine, silky cloud, and then, within an hour, the sun had disappeared, and what it left, its visible traces, was cloud upon cloud illumined by pink flame, radiant, rigid, heavy floods of pink flame against a rich, dark sky.

This was the moment when the breath was suspended, the moment of being snatched up and carried into the pink cloud of flame before the world intervened and, with its inevitable complications and gray banality, corrupted.

She was on her way to T. C.'s to meet Jason. Alan was out of town, and they'd had their first discussion about divorce. Willie and Robin were having dinner at Kay's. Kay had become her ministering angel, so she and Jason would have three, possibly four, hours to be together in this sunstroked paradise, in T. C.'s shack.

She pulled up; Jason's car wasn't there; neither was T. C.'s. During times of turmoil when she'd felt like suicide, she'd come to T. C.'s, where his calmness and joy in living would soothe her, always. "Don't talk like that," T. C. would say. "Long as you got one friend, don' never talk like that. An' you always got me, you got T. C. all the time." She sat on a rusted chair next to T. C.'s door and watched the final fading of the sky into darkness, thinking how unlikely a place this was for her to be sitting, how unlikely that it should have become the center of her life.

She heard his car wind down the road before it pulled into the yard, and just sat there while he got out and came over to her. She was so full of feeling that her body could hardly contain it, fear and foreboding, love and joy, life lived at the edge of disaster.

"Hello, baby."

She stood up. It was dark, and he took her in his arms, and she started crying. He sighed, but he didn't try and stop her. They went in and sat on T. C.'s bed, holding hands and sharing a single cigarette.

"What happened?"

"He was upset, but he finally said if that's what I want . . ."

Jason shook his head. "If you were my wife, if you ever get to be my wife, I'll kill you before I'll let you go."

"I know," she said. "Maybe that's why I'm here, why I have to be with you, because you care so much."

He tossed his hat onto T. C.'s makeshift bureau. "What about the children?"

"We had a hassle about that, but he finally agreed to let me have them as long as he had liberal visitation rights, but he said that he hopes I change my mind about the whole thing."

"I do too."

"You said that before, but you didn't tell me why." She felt hurt and discouraged.

"For all kinds of reasons. You have two children. You need to be married; you need to be married *anyway*; marriage is important. And I can't take care of you. There's so much I want to do for you and so little I can do."

"It doesn't matter," she said.

"It may not now, but it will begin to after a while."

"We can go on this way."

"We could, but it would be better to give each other up."

"I can't give you up. It would be impossible for me unless I went far away, very far away, and it might not even be possible then."

"Last time we talked about this"—he stopped and smiled— "last time, you said you'd kill yourself before you'd give me up."

"Y'know," she said, "you're the only one I know who can do that to me, point out when I've been dramatic and stupid without my resenting it. Anyway, I think one thing one time and another thing another time."

"I know, darlin'," he said. They sat in silence for a moment, and she watched the lighted end of his cigarette, and then he put the cigarette out in a tin can. "I remember when I was a boy and the other boys would talk about the women they were going to have when they got big; I used to think that someday I would have a woman who would love me like no other woman had, and I felt that that would be the woman who was made for me, the woman God intended me to have, and in my imagination she was always white, but her face was never

214

clear, and I never imagined her being anything like you, because there was nothing in my experience to prepare me for someone being like you, especially someone white. After I got grown, I forgot about that dream, and I thought women were just there, beautiful women, to love, to take care of, to make trouble, and for me, white people became simply the incomprehensible enemy. They were there to be dealt with, fought with, spoken with, and sometimes they were there to be taught. If you loved them, it was with the comprehensive love of a Christian. You loved them the way you'd love a crippled dog; in your better moods, you pitied them, and you knew you couldn't expect any more out of them than you were getting. Before I met you, I thought I'd led a pretty full life, I thought I'd done about everything a man could do. I wasn't prepared for you, except by my early boyhood dream, and suddenly that came back to me, and it was almost like a message that came in a dream and said: Connie is the woman who was made for you," his voice in the darkness of the shack, their hands closed together so tightly that they were like one hand, the way their fingers were made so that when they held hands, it was always tightly. "But you were sent to me too late."

"Maybe we weren't ready any earlier."

"Maybe not."

They sat drinking in the darkness, the quietness of their being together almost palpable, an atmosphere to be felt and relaxed into and held. He knew her as no one had ever known her before; it was a strange sensation, being known. It was as if someone had opened your soul like it was a walnut. Now she wanted him to kiss her and hold her so that she wouldn't have to think about the world. She opened her dress, and he kissed her breasts. She finished unbuttoning her dress and stepped out of it. He hung his jacket and tie on T. C.'s clothes pole.

"Y'know," he said, "you an' me, we've gotta be crazy. Come here, Connie, and love me." He held her, held her, held her and kissed her into some new way of feeling beyond where love grew in some shaded grove and out into some hot light of sun and desire and kissing, their mouths . . . until she didn't know anything except the single sensation of wanting to give herself to him so that their bodies became their body became the rivers of the earth.

"I want everything from you," he said, "you know that?"

She nodded. "I want to give you everything."

And when they were in bed, something soft happened, the bed dissolved and slipped away beneath them, and what love was, was the only sound and motion . . . cradled in space where her mind couldn't go, and she'd left her mind somewhere else, and there was the peace and the joy and the ecstasy of their being together in some unknown space of their own love and sensuality. Touch told all, and the mind swam afterward in its own insignificance.

"You know," softly into his ear, "you're worth it all."

"No," he said, half asleep, "we're worth it."

CHAPTER 35

She had made up her mind to leave Alan, definitely, four times. Advice . . . she sought it on every hand. She'd written lengthily to Sally Krause about her problems; she spent half her life, it seemed, on the phone, talking to Kay and Vanessa, and now to Verena, whom she'd told with misgivings, fearing she'd disapprove . . . but she hadn't. She had written to her friend Natasha in San Francisco about the possibility of staying with her and her little girl for a while, until she got her California feet on the ground. The agony of indecision was continual; even when she was absolutely sure that she'd made up her mind, the sureness never lasted more than a day. She'd wake up and lie beside Alan thinking or, now, lie in the bed alone because he was away—what did it all mean? Why couldn't the decision be struck upon her? Why did she have to make it?

She was sitting listening to Mozart that night when he came home. He put down his suitcase and his brief case.

"Hi," he said, "are we supposed to kiss hello any more?"

"I don't know." She could feel age edging into her bones.

"I need a drink," he said. "I don't suppose you'd be willing to fix me one."

She got up. "Sure," she said. "I need one too." Standing over the bar, dropping the ice cubes one by one into the glasses, measuring whiskey, pouring it in, slowly; how much she didn't want to have this conversation. She could feel her strength ebbing away, pressures exerted themselves on her from all sides, and it would be so easy to give in to them, to say: Okay, let's go back to where we were before, forget everything we've learned, and compromise. It would be better for the children . . . maybe . . . but if you honestly believed something was not good for you, how could you think it would be good for your children? One of her friends had said that. And she and Alan whirling off in their different directions, how could that be good for the children?

And she wasn't sure she knew how to go backward . . . and she knew herself . . . she would be bitter always and always wonder who she might have grown into if she'd left him. It would be like saying you didn't have the courage when you needed it . . . and she knew of no way to unlearn the things that Jason had taught her.

"I need time to be by myself and think," she said when she came back into the living room with the drinks.

"Would you like me to leave now?" he asked.

"No." She ignored the irony. "I thought I'd go to New York or Philadelphia in June, just anyplace where I have friends who'd let me stay there and leave me alone for a while. I thought I'd stay a week. Kay said she'd keep the children." The dishonesty of it sliced into her stomach, but she didn't see any other way; she *had* to have some time with Jason.

"*I'll* take care of the kids; you don't have to send them off to Kay. My God, it's like we've been living with your friends all these years. Nothing we do is private."

"I thought you liked Kay."

"I do, but you and I just don't see people in the same way. To me, friends are people you do things with, relax with, drink with. But your notions of friendship are so personal; it's like you want to be living inside other people. You can't accept anything that's comfortable and on the surface, you always have to dig at things." He was getting really angry. She just watched, wondering if that was what it was all about; what else was there but getting inside people—opening up your soul?

"Well, I like being close to people," she said, but she could feel her position being subtly undermined; it was always, it seemed, as if he declared her world unreal; he reminded her of her parents in that: turn the music down, don't become involved in other people's problems, don't get too close to people. But her world was the earth she picked up in her hands, it was the water she swam in, sensation and laughter, dance and the motions of her body.

"But it's impossible to get close to other people," he was yelling at her now. "I know because I tried to get close to you, and see what happened." His face was red, and he banged his glass down on the table. "See what happened!" He picked his glass up again and went out to the bar, presumably to get another drink. She wondered if they were both going insane. Her world with Jason, in the community, with her own children

218

or her dance class had nothing to do with this. Why was she here anyway? How had she ever gotten here?

He came back with straight whiskey. "What I don't understand anyway," he said, "is why I thought we had a good marriage all this time and you suddenly decided we didn't."

"I didn't suddenly decide," she said. "I've felt it a long time. You weren't paying enough attention to notice."

"Oh, *I* was the one who wasn't paying enough attention. You weren't ever here. You were busy putting my children on the picket line, taking them out to meetings or leaving them home and arranging for them to attend black schools."

"Well, well, well. I didn't realize you particularly objected to those things."

"I'm as liberal as you are, Connie, but this is not the way we agreed to live when we got married."

"I wasn't aware that we had an agreement when we got married about how we were going to live. Oh, I know we went through all that love, honor and obey crap, but we were just children when we got married. How did we know how we wanted to live?"

"I knew how *I* wanted to live. I work hard and I want to live well; I want to relax when I get home; I even want to watch television, *color* television, just like the Joneses next door or the Smiths down the street; I like to go to cocktail parties with other intellectuals. I like to vote liberally, give my money to good causes, but I don't feel like I have to give money away all the time to poor, oppressed people. I am a lawyer who supports liberal causes, but I am not a socialist, and I have no desire to be. I would like my wife to be home when I get home; I would like her to be wearing an apron, and I certainly wouldn't mind and would be willing to pay for it if she went to the hairdresser's occasionally. Guitars and dancing are all very well for college, but you are over thirty, Connie."

"I think you have the wrong wife," she said. Her body was cold, she could feel it cold all over. "And you certainly are different from the boy I married."

"I've become a man if that's what you mean." He twirled the ice cubes around in his glass professionally. "I've gotten over my little-boy notions that the world is out there to change. You radicals and artsy-craftsy types are all the same. You're not in college any more, Connie, don't you see that? Civil-rights demonstrations and folk singing are the way kids do things. Grownups become part of the establishment, go to cocktail parties, play golf, change things slowly from within and make suitable friends. They acquire property and make statements on the radio. They wear ties and jackets, and speak nicely to people who can help them get ahead."

She sat back sullenly in her chair; she could feel the tears in her eyes. He had changed. She had not changed? What had she done? What was the difference between the ways in which they had changed?

"You're not the right wife for me," he said then, "clearly. You just won't grow up and become rational. You're too emotional. Emotion is for children and hysterical radicals. At any rate"—he looked at her as if she was in the witness chair and he was cross-examining her—"I have the feeling that you're more interested in another man than you are in me."

The tears ran down her face, and she nodded.

"It's T. C., isn't it?"

She shook her head. Why would he think that?

"Well that's where you spend all your time. Who is it?"

"I don't want to tell you." She was crying hard now.

"Why not? I'm not going to do anything about it. I just think it's fair for me to know."

"It's Reverend Williams." She knew that Jason would never understand in a million years why she had told him. But it was fair, Alan was right about that.

"That's too bad," he said.

"What do you mean?" She had the feeling of impending insanity again.

"I had a lot of respect for that man."

She wondered what he meant; she was just crying now, sobbing, the sounds shaking her.

"Is he planning to marry you?" the lawyer's voice again.

She shook her head.

"Well, that's just great." He got up and went into the bar

again for whiskey. "Just great." She heard him from the other room.

She was still sitting in the chair when he came back, sitting with her head on her lap and her arms locked around her knees; her tears had stopped, and she thought she must be half asleep and half crazy; he tapped her on the shoulder, and she sat up. He had salami sandwiches in his hands, salami sandwiches with lettuce and mayonnaise on poppy-seed rolls, the way they always ate them. She felt almost like laughing.

"Want a salami sandwich?"

She nodded and took one.

"Look, Connie," he said when he was seated again, "if he's not going to marry you, why don't you just try to stay here. Marriage is, you know, permanent, and a divorce is not going to be that good for my career. And what difference could it possibly make to you, if he's not willing to marry you. What does he want anyway?" a sudden flash of anger.

"He wants me to stay with you."

"Well then." He smiled, and the lawyer emerged, triumphant in the courtroom. "What possible question can there be?"

"It's not what *I* want." She was crying again; why couldn't she stop crying, why couldn't she be like him? "It's not what *I* think is best, for me or the kids, or for you ultimately. It just won't work."

And that was the moment at which she knew that the decision had really been made and that nothing could change it.

CHAPTER 36

The campaign was much more difficult than she'd known it would be. In the first place they had no money, and so the campaign committee took to the streets collecting nickels and quarters and dimes from people in the black community. They also went to the university campus and tried to collect large pledges from the professors and got a few and didn't get a lot more.

The speed and confusion with which Connie was living made her feel like someone had put her on a circular track and was running her around and around. The campaign was pressure, pure and simple. The cops had always known his car, but now they followed it everywhere. . . . The first black man in the county since Reconstruction to run for the commission, a milestone . . . And at home there was pressure. Because Alan knew now that she was really leaving. There was pressure inside herself. She was trying to launch herself out onto open waters because she wanted to do something she couldn't do and couldn't bring herself to do the thing she was supposed to do. The question the figures in her fantasy world put to her continually was: What right do you have? And the question tore her mind apart, and she carried a sickening weight with her everywhere because she was, after all, making a heavy decision by herself for the three of them: Willie, Robin, herself, and indirectly for Alan. But her instincts told her that Alan would be all right; she felt that more distinctly than she felt that she would be all right.

Night, a campaign meeting at Vanessa's, and the day's progression had been even faster than she'd expected it to be. They had postponed the dance performance, but they still rehearsed; she had had a rehearsal after she'd gone out to collect money for the campaign, then she'd played with the kids, made dinner, and now there were the dishes. She hadn't studied, and she had a quiz in the morning. Alan was gathering together the papers he needed to put in his brief case, and in the pocket of the soft, silky dress she'd bought for Jason's campaign was a letter from Sally Krause that she hadn't had time to read. She'd been waiting for this letter ever since she'd written to Sally about

223

Jason, yet she was afraid to open it. She and Sally grew close and then distant and then close again, but, for as long as she could remember, she had respected Sally's opinions. From the living room, she could hear the sounds of "I Love Lucy," and through the door she could see her two children sitting like two soft dolls that someone had dumped in front of the TV. They sat transfixed, their round little backs toward her, Robin's hair curling down onto her shoulders. Connie sighed, letting her breath out slowly, and felt the response from her deeper soul, something shuddering and frightened. What she saw in her house: warm lamplight, a man standing in front of his desk, two children watching television, herself washing dishes. What she heard in her house: water running, papers being shuffled, Lucy yelling at Ricky and crying. She wanted it all to mean what it might to a casual stranger looking at it, but she was the stranger to it in its present form. Her children were her home, Jason was her home, and before she'd known Jason, she had had no home in that sense.

"Good-bye, I'll see you later."

"Okay. Have a good class."

"Bye, Daddy," and she watched him bend to kiss them, ruffle Robin's hair. And as she turned back to the sink, she could feel her tears starting. Jason said: Stay there, baby. Don't break up your home. And all that was most hungry in her for home listened, but you could probably only live for an entire lifetime in a situation that stifled you if you didn't know it stifled you. The decision had been made, but she could feel that she was only slowly learning to live into it. . . .

"Willie!"

He didn't move.

"Willie, Will-ee."

Finally: "Yes, Mama."

"Come here."

He came backward, watching the TV.

"Alma's coming in a few minutes. I'll be at a meeting. I want you to take charge of you and Robin for Alma. You get un-dressed, and then you can have some milk and a doughnut. And be in bed by eight-thirty."

"Okay, Mama. Can we watch TV until eight-thirty?"
"Yes, if you're undressed and ready for bed."
"Okay."

At Vanessa's they sat around the living room, on the couch, in chairs, on the floor, and the turbulence within her lay for a moment calmed. Jason sat in a large armchair making notes on the thick pad in his lap, beatific looking; T. C. was on the couch putting spoonful after spoonful of sugar into his coffee. Kay Levy and Alice Rivers were there and two preachers from out in the county who were going to help organize the small towns. Everything seemed to Connie lucid and beautiful, and the lamplight in Vanessa's living room was soft enough so that it was as if each face had been dipped in it, and the planes and shadows were evident, and each face had a soft, rubbed look. Peace. So Connie took out her letter from Sally Krause and put it on the floor in front of her to read.

Dear Connie,
My God! I am totally and wildly overwhelmed. The wilde, wilde Connie Bartlett Wilder. And I thought it was all over. I thought you'd settled. But God—a preacher? You and a preacher, hardened old atheist you. I know ten people who will die of unbelief (a new kind) when I tell them.

So after all that flippancy, you are saying (ache, ache), what do I really think? Because, *tout compris*, you wouldn't have written me if you didn't really want to know what I think.

Well, really, seriously, I think you're making a terrible mistake. My latest and most deft and complicated shrink (a beautiful man) is very big on the ties that bind. You have, after all, two children and your husband. Alan, has, after all, been a good husband, which I am gathering from my multidivorced friends is very rare. Living, mind orientation (IQ height), children, so-phis-tee-cation. All are there. I don't know. Your name, after all, is Constance. I can scarcely imagine you any more. What are you looking like?

My shrink, Edouard LeBlanc (Dr. Edward White to the un-initiated, who see him not as White riding on a black charger to my rescue) has advised me repeatedly to form some ties. He thinks I am rootless. Does he leer in my direction? Not yet, but who knows what the future will bring. All of which only leads me in my usual ineptly tactless way to say that I don't think you should leave Alan and that, as far as the preacher goes, I think you should keep yourself safe, which I rather suppose means to give him up.

At any rate, what kind of relationship can you possibly have? My shrink says that the best marriages and amours are made with the people next door. Shrewd, yes, you are. He grew up five blocks from me in San Francisco.

Yet, yet, I'm not kidding. I think if you leave Alan, you will regret it forever. Of course, we must always remember that I've never been married and therefore should not presume to judge . . . etc. . . . etc.

and love,
Sally

P.S. Write me developments.

She folded the letter in a tiny packet and put it back in her pocket. Then she looked at the faces around the room again, all changed, as if a hammer blow had been dealt to her world, and she knew that now, for this moment, she couldn't stay here. She got up and walked out the door and down the stairs and out the downstairs door, and could feel the tears streaming down her face. She felt Jason look at her as she passed him, but once she was downstairs, as she went through the downstairs door, she could hear his voice, calm and even, and then suddenly the dark cool air of the night became the atmosphere that she could feel her problems fit into as if they were so many night clouds, and in a moment, there was a rectangle of light where the door had closed behind her, and she heard Kay's voice:

"Connie?" tentative, full of compassion. Kay was only five feet away from her.

"I don't need anybody," and she could feel the tears pouring down her face; it was as if she were drowning in them; they had been going on a long time. Kay looked at her for a moment and then turned around and went back into the house. And the rectangle of light became a thin line, and then there was darkness.

She walked in the street for twenty minutes. For him to walk out of that meeting to find her would be disaster for him, she knew that, but all she wanted was for him to stand in the middle of the street with her and hold her until she stopped crying.

Finally calm, she went back in, and no one gave more than the flicker of a suggestion, even by their expressions, that she'd done anything even slightly unusual, and she felt grateful and went into the kitchen with Vanessa to pour coffee and set the doughnuts out on plates.

And outside, in that cool darkness which was their medium and their veil, she stood next to his car and gave him some papers that she had typed for him, so that they could speak for a moment, almost privately. And one by one, the other cars pulled away.

"What happened to you tonight, honey?" his voice gentle and weary.

"I read a letter from a friend of mine, and she told me I was all wrong. She told me to give you up and stay with Alan and what kind of relationship could we have anyway."

He sighed. "Your friend cannot possibly know about our relationship. No one can understand our relationship except us. Now go home and sleep, honey. I'll call you tomorrow."

"Okay," she said, and went to her car. The authority in his voice; she loved the way he said things, the depth of his belief in what he said.

And, at home, she sat at the kitchen table, her legs on the rung of the kitchen chair, doing her Latin. Sitting with the Latin dictionary open before her, picking out obscure meanings, translating from one language to another as if all her life had been the calm, cool pursuit of the solutions to intellectual puzzles.

CHAPTER 37

It was the night before the election, his last rally, out in one of the country towns. Just before dusk, she drove out of Orangedale into the country feeling the pressure lessen, feeling the weight of the tangle of trees overhead blunt the edges of her feelings but also feeling the beginnings of excitement. He'd kept her away from the rallies, and she'd had the sense that he felt they might be dangerous and something more . . . as if he withheld from her some piece of information that he felt she might not be ready to handle.

The country town she drove into was Grady, population twelve hundred, and she asked at the first corner she hit how to get to the city park, and the man laughed and said he reckoned as how she couldn't miss it if she went straight ahead and turned right on Main Street, at the first and only traffic light in town. She drove slowly; it was like Orangedale but without the university and all the stores. It seemed like a town in another country.

And then she got close to the park. Hundreds of cars were parked for blocks each way, and in the block of the park itself, they were double parked. Through the open car window, she could smell beer and barbecue, and the clear heat of the early evening sharpened the voices, loud, white Southern voices, and overhead there were lights, hot, square stadium lights, and she could hear laughter and then the blaring of a loudspeaker:

"Aw raht, everyone, we're gonna have the campaign speeches now."

She got out of her car and walked very slowly toward the folding chairs where everyone was sitting. The scene was memories to her, but memories that were not her own, memories of novels she had read, of settings in which men were lynched, and she could feel a shudder down her spine, not her memories but his, and she saw him sitting in the front row, with T. C. by his side . . . and they were the only black people there. She walked to the back of the rows of folding chairs and stood looking at the whole scene: women in cotton dresses, men in jeans and slacks and short-sleeved shirts, children running around, groups of people talking, closely knit, conspiratorial.

In Orangedale they were able, at least to some extent, to live within the illusion of an integrated world that they had created; they had their meetings, they went to each other's houses, they all ate together in public places, and their illusion was so strong that it created an atmosphere of reality that extended beyond them. That atmosphere was, of course, dissipated when she and Jason tried to go out in public, but here . . . here there would be no possibility even of living within the illusion . . . you could feel past patterns claiming the present in the chairs you sat in, hear it in voices and see it in the way people spoke to each other.

"The first candidate, our own Mistah Wilson," and there was much applause. She half-listened to him, but she waited for Jason. He said he had no chance of winning but that they had made their impression; the first black man to run for the commission since Reconstruction would be remembered.

Finally he got up. "On my way here this evening," he began, "as I was driving through the black community, I stopped and asked a man where the park was where they were holding the rally tonight, and he was not even aware that there was a rally being held in Grady tonight." He paused. "The reason that I decided to run for the county commission was because many people, many white people, that is, feel that black people are not interested in the government of the county, and this is not the case. The reason that I decided to run for the county commission is because I am concerned about the government of this county. I have been a resident of this county for forty-two years, and I am concerned about the way in which the land is being developed in this county. I am concerned about the transportation problems in the county and the utility problems. I am concerned about the problems of the farmers and I am concerned about the problems of the poor. I come here tonight as a representative of those citizens who wish to see this county progress, but I also come here as a representative of my race, and in that capacity, I wonder about the man who didn't know that the rally was here tonight, and I wonder why he didn't feel that it was his business to know about it. Was it laziness that stopped him from taking his rightful part in political life, or was it perhaps fear? Some of my people are very old-fashioned"—he stopped and looked over his audience—"and they think that white people still want to deny them their rights, but I have the chance to move from place to place; I travel all over the United States to conferences. As a minister, that is part of my job, and I have the chance to *see* what is taking place in this country, and I know that all over the country, and all over the South in particular, people are coming to realize that we must work together in order to make this country into a democracy. I would appreciate being one of your county commissioners," and he sat down, and to Connie's surprise, they clapped, and the applause was more than polite. Connie got up and went to her car. She didn't want to hear the others; she wanted to get away. Starting the motor, the sound almost a violation of the stillness because hers was the first motor to start . . . she felt a thousand aches, pride in him, loneliness and the beginnings of nostalgia for the world he inhabited, which she must leave if she went to San Francisco . . . time and the tides of being, none of it made sense.

The next evening, they sat in Vanessa's living room and listened to the returns, sat drinking coffee and smoking while it became increasingly clear that Jason had lost. He had talked to her a lot about how you had to deal with things you wanted and didn't get, losses, what some people termed failures, but she had never seen him lose before. Now he sat, unperturbed, smoking, laughing with Horn and T. C. She was more upset than he was. The announcer introduced a candidate for the school board who was about to make a concession speech.

"You could do that," Connie said. "Go on the radio and make a concession speech."

He laughed. "I ain't conceding nothing. Maybe that's because I'm a nigger."

T. C. roared.

"But we've lost this, honey," Jason a moment later. "This is really over."

She sighed and snapped off the radio.

Two days later, the paper published an editorial commending

Reverend Williams on his campaign and extending the heart-felt hope that he would not lose interest in politics because he had lost, and would run again the next time.

Two days later, Connie found out that Reverend Williams' wife was going to Philadelphia to the conference with him. However, he said that they could have some time together. And so she decided to go anyway.

CHAPTER 38

He got tied up and couldn't meet her at the airport, as he'd promised. There were so many white people at the airport and almost no black people. She had never known there were so many white people. Everywhere she went in the airport, they had taken it over. Occasionally there would be a black clerk behind a desk, occasionally a black passenger, none of them him. She looked for hats, for his dark, serious, brooding face.

Later, she mentioned it to him: "There were so many white people at the airport."

"There are so many white people, baby, in the world." And for a moment she could see it all from his point of view; the white people hadn't taken over the airport; they'd always had it; it was one of their occupied territories. . . .

The five days slid out of their grasp . . . they knew the value of an hour, a minute, even a second in a way that people seldom did, rarely had to, but still time passed. . . . Late Saturday afternoon, they were lying on the huge bed watching the sun burn lower over the city . . . they were high above the city streets and kept the curtains open.

"Does it mean something to you to say that I always thought my life would be memorable for me at its end only because of the work I'd done, but that because of you it will be memorable because I have experienced more joy than most men are given."

"It means a lot, but I wanted . . ." She could feel her voice choking.

"Shhh." He put two fingers to her lips. "I believe that I know everything you've wanted. I only wish I had the power to give it all to you."

"I know," and she lay in his arms, letting the moment stand for absolute peace; when she said "I know," her head told her heart to learn, to start to learn that he would not always be there with her, that in three months time, they were putting a country between them.

Summer in the Orangedale heat . . . she finished her thesis before the end of June. She and Alan made casual but practical plans to get their divorce within the year. Her friend Natasha

233

wrote that they should come to San Francisco; her house was large, and they could stay until they got settled. Certainly Connie would be able to get a job typing or something, and then, with her master's degree, she would find something better in time.

And so she felt that the practical arrangements were being made. It was the arrangement of her heart within her body that was giving her trouble. She was leaving not only Jason but also a place where she had lots of friends, a place where, in some complex, elusive way, people seemed to understand her. She was going to her beloved Bay area, where the life she would lead must be utterly different, and the person she had become—how would that person lead that life?

It was a mechanical summer. The heat tightened everything up, and she felt herself tighten in response. She did things mechanically, let the children play with their friends and entertain each other. Alan moved out. She devoted time to working with her dance class, losing her sense of herself as she sharpened their technique for what she regarded as the group's final concert.

"I will come back," she would say to Jason more and more often as the summer progressed, as the day on which they were to leave drew closer.

"Don't promise," he said. "I couldn't stand it if you promised and didn't come back. You don't have any idea what you're going to do. It's impossible to plan that far ahead."

"I do know," she said, "I do," knowing she didn't.

She ate almost nothing that summer; she lived on grape drink, which the children drank with every meal, and chocolate bars, which she purchased at the grocery store when she felt weak.

"You *look* great," Kay told her, "but you're so thin, and I know you're not great, so it comes out that you're worrying me to death," and she laughed unhappily.

"All you need is one fren'," T. C. at the bus station. "An' you always got ol' T. C. Don' need nothin' more, but you gotta

234

eat, young lady, you gotta eat to live. Now jes' let me order you some eggs and grits while the children have their ice cream," but even when he ordered it, she couldn't eat more than five or six mouthfuls, and he had to finish it. There seemed to be no way of getting the food from her mouth to her stomach; it would just sit there in her mouth, and she'd chew and chew, but she couldn't make the muscles work that would take it down to her stomach, and she couldn't make her appetite exist, and once each day, someone would say something to her that would make her leave a room and go off and cry, or sometimes no one would say anything to trigger it; it would just happen. She might be watching the sun stain the leaves on a tree outside the window, and she might think of T. C.'s, and the tears would start. She did not know that human beings had that many tears to give.

She thought of suicide, but she had children to raise. Besides, she might see him again; he might come to visit her in California. Besides, there was no need to commit suicide; she was already dead; it was just a matter of their carrying her dead body off to California, that separation which is final, eternal. "But I will come back," she said to him in each phone conversation, and imagined herself in a huge, almost airless vault with steel walls. I will get out, it is the will that counts, the will itself is enough . . . she hoped.

She did community work. She collected people and carried them in her car—to the grocery store, to register to vote, to see the girls in the reform school. She tried to keep the children busy, herself simply in motion. If she could have spent that entire summer in her car, she might have staved off some of the pain. Or so she told herself.

The heat drenched them, kept them sweaty and sticky and in need of water. "I'll be glad when we go to California," Willie said. "It's too hot here." She started crying when he said that; there was no stopping her. Long afterward, she would remember that as the summer she spent crying.

Kay took them to the swimming pool, and she dove deep, deep under water, almost as if she hoped each time that she might never come up; it was clean and fresh under water, and life was as simple and clean as that passage of water you dove through. Kay planned things for them to do, and Verena planned things for them to do, and she went to each of the planned things, a wooden figure in their midst.

Jason said: "We've got to taper off. We should stop making love now so that it won't be so hard on us when you go."

"No." She clung to him. "We have plenty of time *not* to make love while I'm in California. We should pack in as much as we can now."

"That's *your* idea," softly.

She would wake in the morning with a sick sensation filling her. Sometimes, briefly, in the oblivion of the night, she could forget what it was that kept her disturbed, but then, with the rising of each sun, she would remember, and the sick sensation would relocate itself in every cell of her body, and she would wonder how she could possibly get through another day.

The night they met for the last time, there was almost an element of relief in it. They spent the first hour of their time talking about what they would do in California, building it up, enchanting it to the tune of their desires.

"I can't say anything to you except that I love you as I've never loved another human being." He took her in his arms and just held her there; before there had been any sex, there had always been this love; it had been there before either one of them was born; it had been there just waiting for them. "When I drop you off at your car, I'm going to kiss you once, and then I want you to get out without saying anything. Anything you need to say then, you'd better write me, because otherwise I won't be able to stand it and I won't let you go. Do you understand?"

She nodded, feeling her throat ache, feeling her whole face strain with the effort of not crying.

"Will you do it for me?"

She nodded again.

"I've made you a tape of some of my feelings. You can listen to it in California. I want to be sure you know everything that I feel for you, but I can't tell you now."

They drove the dark roads, back through the tunnel of trees and down the main road, a tangle of storm-tossed trees, each tree a landmark in her life, each tree as familiar as a line on her hand. He stopped the car, and he kissed her, and she got out.

She sat in her car and played his tape:

I am a black man, one who has never regretted being black, although I've regretted the penalties and injuries that have come with being black and have suffered my people's pain. . . . I didn't expect to ever love anyone the way I love Connie, especially a white girl, but Connie is . . . it's whatever it is that's deep down in her soul that makes her what she is. . . .

Sobs broke out of her body like animals out of cages, fierce and willing and somehow having nothing to do with her. The crying came from a part of her that was new and open and vulnerable, those depths untouched before he came.

And she was leaving tomorrow . . . Connie, we talk of California, but we may never see each other again. She knew that she would love him forever, but that was all she knew.

The world is too little in the face of us.

They loved each other, and the world had many axes to grind and bring down upon their heads. All they asked for was a corner where she could tie her hair back and make him eggs and grits in the morning, a corner where they could raise her two children and one of their own, a corner where, at the sound of a voice or a distant door closing or the creaking of a screen, they wouldn't have to leap out of bed and dress in fear.

The rest of their lives would go to God and to Jason's people, the dark people, the thirteenth tribe of Israel. It was a vision of order she had in her head, an order of the heart that would be a kind of absolute complement to the chaos they had lived through together. He had answers to chaos, answers in his strong hands, in the arms he raised in blessing above the heads of his people. . . .

We are too little in the face of the world.

However big their love, they would disrupt, wound, shatter wherever they went; they would leave behind them a trail of people angered and saddened because they found their only peace lying in each other's arms.

She walked the streets of the city, and she carried his face everywhere. She walked, enveloped in his atmosphere, alone, on her lunch hour and sometimes late at night when the kids were in bed and Natasha was watching them.

She looked at the faces of white men, and they seemed to her paper thin. Beneath their superficial sense of calmness and security lay traces of bigotry, real or suspected; at the very least, in most of them, lay an unwillingness to commit themselves to faces not of their own color. Suspicion she'd learned from being briefly and tentatively inside the black culture.

She looked at the faces of black men, and occasionally across one of them, she would see a flicker of resemblance pass. But it passed. His passion, his eyes in love, in wonder and revelation stayed burned into her brain. In other faces, she detected weakness and felt, time after time, a basic disillusionment. In his, she felt his power to rise, transcendent, above the heads of the people, his feet barely touching the tops of the pews. . . .

Walking on pews . . .
Walking on water . . .

In no other face did eyes burn so, the power and the glory, amen. She walked the streets searching faces, turning corners hoping that she might meet his spirit briefly garbed in flesh. The spirit and the substance, the body and the soul. But nowhere along the dark, windy streets of the city, nowhere could she find him.